Terrace Books, a trade imprint of the University of Wisconsin Press, takes its name from the Memorial Union Terrace, located at the University of Wisconsin–Madison. Since its inception in 1907, the Wisconsin Union has provided a venue for students, faculty, staff, and alumni to debate art, music, politics, and the issues of the day. It is a place where theater, music, drama, literature, dance, outdoor activities, and major speakers are made available to the campus and the community. To learn more about the Union, visit www.union.wisc.edu.

Meet Me Halfway

Milwaukee Stories

Jennifer Morales

Terrace Books
A trade imprint of the University of Wisconsin Press

Publication of this volume has been made possible, in part,
through support from the Brittingham Fund.

Terrace Books
A trade imprint of the University of Wisconsin Press
1930 Monroe Street, 3rd Floor
Madison, Wisconsin 53711-2059
uwpress.wisc.edu

3 Henrietta Street, Covent Garden
London WC2E 8LU, United Kingdom
eurospanbookstore.com

Printed in the United States of America

Library of Congress Cataloging-in-Publication Data

Morales, Jennifer (Writer), author.
[Short stories. Selections]
Meet me halfway: Milwaukee stories / Jennifer Morales.
    pages   cm
ISBN 978-0-299-30364-8 (pbk.: alk. paper)
ISBN 978-0-299-30363-1 (e-book)
1. Milwaukee (Wis.)—Fiction.   2. Race relations—Fiction.   I. Title.
PS3613.O666A6   2015
813'.6—dc23
2014030802

A version of "He___ ___ ___ ___ (2010) and a ver___ n of "Got the Ball"
appeared in Tem____ ___ (Winter 2013).

This is a work o___ ___. Names, characters, businesses, and places are eith___ ___he products of the
author's imagin___ ___ ___ ___ ___tional characters to
actual persons, l___ ng or dead, is purely coincidental. Any historical event d___ ___cted in the work is
also used in a fi___ ___ ___ ___l representation of
such event.

If I ever had to leave Alabama,
I'd want to live on the south side
of Milwaukee.

Alabama Governor George Wallace,
launching his 1964 presidential campaign

Contents

Acknowledgments

The children of Milwaukee are the reason I wrote this book. Their struggles, discoveries, and resilience in this difficult place compelled me to try to pin some of Milwaukee's voices down, to listen and maybe sound out something about how this city came to be the way it is.

I'm very grateful to the youth with whom or for whom I have had the privilege to work, as a member of the Milwaukee school board, a community activist, a Sunday school teacher, or a visiting writer in the schools. They have taught me so much about what it means to bloom where you're planted, especially when somebody's always stepping on your leaves.

I'm also blessed to have been Mom, Jamma, or Auntie to other Milwaukee kids: the ones I gave birth to, Anansi and Cedro, of course, but also Dominique, Felicia, Jeremy, Angelica, Charisma, Johnny, Jenna, Dominique Jr., and important friends Trajan, Angelo, Arri, Evan, and the students of the Alliance School. No education could be more powerful than the one I've received doing my small part to help you come up in this world. Thank you.

I'm grateful for the patience and wisdom of my teachers at Antioch University, especially Dodie Bellamy, Gayle Brandeis, Tananarive Due, Steve Heller, Alistair McCartney, and Alma Luz Villanueva, who provided many insights on early versions of this text. I had the great fortune to be a member of Antioch's Carnelian MFA cohort and, as I worked on this book, my clever "Carnies" offered me a generous supply of editorial advice, compassionate butt-kicking, and timely comic relief. I'm especially thankful for the friendship and keen talents of Jenn Crowell, Pazit Cahlon, Heather Mingus, Kristen Forbes, LeVan Hawkins, Philip Barragan, Elaina Ellis, and (Carnie-by-association) Dasha Kelly.

There are simply no words to thank the members of my Milwaukee writing group. They were often the first readers of these stories and the first to meet these characters. Ellen Bravo, Rachel Buff, and Patty Donndelinger have been brilliant colleagues in this work and ardent advocates for a wider audience for it. I offer a special thank you to Rachel, who knocked on (and possibly down) several doors to get this book on its way to publication. Thanks also to local readers Lesley Salas, Dale Weiss, Tina Owen, and Deaduri Gales, and to Barbara Miner, who lifted up the Governor Wallace quote that serves as the epigraph.

Many publishers have shied away from books that deal with race. I'm inspired by the board and staff of the University of Wisconsin Press for having the *ganas* to champion this one. I'm particularly indebted to Raphael Kadushin for his engagement and advocacy.

Finally, I must acknowledge the support of Keren Lee Orr. She bought me rounds of darts when the going was hard and celebratory drinks when it was not. I am so grateful that when I step away from my writing, I walk into the comfort of her sweet companionship.

Meet Me Halfway

Heavy Lifting

Johnquell's neck is broken and chances are he won't walk again. I had asked him to move a bookcase and told him I'd give him a few bucks. I thought he could use it. I was right and I usually am about them. He was a good enough kid, I guess. None too bright, but willing to take on a task now and then that an old lady can't do for herself, like trim the evergreen hedges in front of the picture window, or haul furniture out of the basement and to the curb, things like that. The way the economy's been, even those broken end tables and that old sofa went before the garbagemen could take them away. I watch from the living room, so I know. Some man saw the end tables Walt and I bought in 1967—the tables were Thonet and still looked good, so even the garbage pickers could tell it was of a certain quality—sitting a little lopsided on the curb, and the rattletrap station wagon slowed down for a look and sure as I'm sitting here the better of the two tables was gone not two minutes after Johnquell put it out.

People have been hurting. Milwaukee's not what it used to be, that's for sure. Most of our old friends sold their homes here the minute they could find a buyer, back in the '70s when the integration got going. We might have gone out to the suburbs ourselves, if it hadn't been for Walt's job at the city water works and the residency requirement. It seemed like a decent exchange at the time. He was making good money and it seemed like, as crazy as some of that Black Panther business had been, and the riots and what have you, it was going to pass. Everybody knew that some neighborhoods were ours and some were theirs and it would all work itself out. It was going to be OK.

Walt's been dead twelve years now and the three before that hardly count. He was at St. Eugene's, staring out his window over the roses lining the parking lot. I'd come in and ask what he was staring at and he'd just say, "I'm waiting for someone." I could never get him to tell me who. It must not have been me.

Most women of my age, the ones I see at church and bingo anyway, they always use some kind of fancy phrase talking about their dead husbands. I don't go in for that "he passed on" or "he's deceased" stuff, myself. He's dead and that's probably a good thing, if you ask me. His mind was already long gone when his heart gave out at St. Eugene's. Didn't even recognize his own wife of forty-seven years. That's dead.

So for a long time there hasn't been anybody to help with the heavy lifting. Spencer, my no-good son, lives in Ohio. Don't ask what got him to move to Columbus, Ohio. It was some woman, Lori or Laura or Loreen. Can't remember. She's run off, too, but he stays out there, working for UPS. The girls are here, but they're girls. So I asked John-quell to come over, to move the bookcase from the living room to the spare room on the second floor.

I didn't like the bookcase where it was anymore. It didn't used to lean the way it did lately. I sat there at night under my reading lamp, with the TV on low and looking at catalogs or the *Reader's Digest*, and I'd look up and there would be the bookcase leaning over me, like it might topple on my head. I haven't pulled a book off those shelves in at least fifteen years, only dusted around them when I had to, so it wouldn't bother me at all if it went upstairs, in the back of the house, in the spare room that used to be Spencer's.

I saw Johnquell's mother outside on her back porch on Friday after-noon. She was in a folding chair with her feet up on a five-gallon pickle bucket, just staring into the alley. She was wearing her office clothes except she must have swapped her work shoes for the slippers she had on over her dark nylons. She was ignoring a couple of bees swarming her, drinking something out of a red plastic cup with some kind of cartoon character on it. Must have been one of her little relatives' cups. She's got so many of them—nieces, nephews, cousins, I don't know who—that when there is a barbecue, I can't even go out onto my own porch or I'll be mobbed by those little urchins demanding a popsicle or what have you. They're always begging. I said to Mrs. (is she a Mrs.?—I never knew) Braxton, "Do you think Johnquell would like to come over tomorrow and move a bookcase?"

Mrs. Braxton squinted up into my yard, where I was standing, leaning over the wrought iron railing on my back stoop. I tried to be neighborly but I really didn't know how to talk to her. The message always seemed to come out wrong somehow, like there was a big canyon between our houses that you couldn't shout across without the echo screwing up what you were trying to say.

She said, "I'll let him know you asked," turned back to look at the alley, and that was that. She had a round face that looked kind but could turn hard all of a sudden—not so much angry or hostile, but un-interested, like the girl at the grocery store checkout who says what she needs to say just to move you along.

Johnquell—where do they come up with these names?—must have said yes because he came by Saturday morning first thing. I say "first thing" because for him it clearly was. I'd been up since six and it was nearly 10:00 a.m. He was wearing those long basketball shorts and tube socks with slip-on sandals, like he was heading for the shower, not a neighbor's house. He was a big child, with his mother's round face and dark skin. He must have been seventeen years old or so but tall and built like a Clydesdale. If I saw him at night on the street I would faint right there. Here in my living room, though, it was alright; he was just the boy from next door.

I showed him the bookcase. It's four feet tall, solid oak, two and a half feet across and every inch of it loaded with paperbacks—my romances mostly, plus some of those histories Walt always liked. I told him which room he should bring it to and he bent down to pick it up.

"Now, wait," I said. "Don't you want to get the books off first?"

"Naw," he said. "It's easier this way." So, you can see, the whole thing was really his fault.

Johnquell scooted between the wall and the bookcase and picked it up by the middle, tipping it back so the books would stay in place on their way up the stairs, his chin hooked over the top edge to hold it steady. He made a face at me then. I'm not sure if it was a smirk, like he was saying, "See? I can do this," or it was just from the effort of carrying it, but I gave him an encouraging smile. His big, brown eyes still had some sleep in them.

I stood at the foot of the stairs, as if I was any help standing there twisting the edge of my housecoat. "Are you sure?" I said, when he was four steps up. There were fourteen steps altogether. I know because I've lived here for fifty-seven years so I've been up and down them a few times—babies, laundry, all the daily comings and goings.

When we bought the house Walt picked me up and carried me over the threshold and then right up those stairs to our new bedroom. He was so strong then and I was a just a little wisp of a thing. We had moved into the back room of his parents' house on the south side when we were first married. He sure didn't see the point in carrying me over the threshold there and setting me down on the dingy linoleum in their foyer. I understood what he meant. Living with his parents, it was like we were just playing at being married, never mind Father Wysocki's "man-and-wife" hoopla. The cramped quarters are probably why Nancy, the first of the three babies, didn't come along until we were in a house of our own.

Those stairs are ruined for me now. I heard it, the crack. They say that the person it happens to doesn't hear it, or doesn't remember it, anyway. But I will, for the rest of my life.

He fell in slow motion. He must have knocked the bookcase into the wall at the turn in the stairs, because just a second after he began the turn, he came falling backward, like in slow motion, as I said, though the whole event didn't last but a minute, I guess. He fell onto his back and slid down a few steps, his chin still hooked over the edge, and he came crashing to a halt not two feet from the floor, the weight of all those books snapping his neck like a stick.

I ran to the living room for the phone and called 911. I'm not sure I made myself clear to the operator. I think she thought I had fallen down the stairs and still somehow could talk on the phone.

"Johnquell," I said. "A boy, a black boy," but I could tell she was already radioing the ambulance. She wasn't paying any attention to me.

I went back to the stairs. I was nervous because I didn't know what I would find there and I was right to be. Johnquell was on his back, the bookcase still under his chin, and blood was running out his nose and around his mouth. His eyes were wide and I remember thinking even then how white they seemed against his dark skin. His hands had let loose their grip and while I stood there trying to figure out what more I could do, the hand nearer to me slid like a pound of meat down onto the carpeted stairs with a thud that made my stomach turn.

"Oh, why don't they hurry?" I said.

I tried to keep a certain distance. I was worried that if I touched him I might hurt him more. Instead, I started taking the books out of the bookcase and stacking them on the steps above him. I thought it would help, lightening the load.

Johnquell snorted, sneezed almost, and a fresh flow of blood came coursing up his face and onto the beige stair runner. He was breathing at least.

"Are you OK, Johnquell? John?" I said. "It's going to be alright. It is. The ambulance is coming." I said these things, trying to comfort him and myself. His eyes were unfocused, so different from the light in them just a few minutes before. I touched his brow for just a second but the blood was pooling around his head and the sight of it made the room spin. I turned away and picked more books out of the case, top shelf first, because I thought that's where most of the pressure would be.

I thought about his mother, right next door, not knowing what was happening. Maybe she was watching TV. Maybe she was doing laundry. I didn't have her phone number. She would know something was wrong when the ambulance came. She would come out of the house and come running toward my door, shouting.

The ambulance arrived and I opened the door to the paramedics—two big men, one black and one white—and then I stood out of the way.

"Aw, jeez," the white paramedic hissed.

"Hang in there, man," said the black one, as the two of them worked together to lift the bookcase off of Johnquell and stand it, upside down, at the foot of the stairs.

The white one talked into a walkie-talkie on his shoulder and a second later the ambulance driver appeared with a big plastic board.

"How'd it happen?" he asked the other two, but I answered, because how would they know?

"He carried the bookcase up. I don't read those books anymore. I wanted it in Spencer's old room. He hit the wall and came back down on his back. It hit him . . ." I thought I should continue, explain about the money, the cracking sound, his mother, but all the whys and hows were getting mixed up in my head and I just felt so tired.

The two paramedics looked at each other for a second and then the black one said, "It's OK, ma'am. We're going to take this guy in and get him fixed up, so don't you worry."

They must have been talking to me and working to get Johnquell onto the board at the very same time because, next thing I knew, they were carrying him out. He was crying but not making any noise. I touched his arm as he went by.

It wasn't his mother who came out of the house next door but one of his sisters, the tallest one—Johnqueitha or Johneitha—I can't remember these names. She ran for the back of the ambulance and then I saw her make a dash for the front door of their house, shout something to someone inside, and run back to jump into the ambulance. A moment later, one of the younger sisters appeared at the door, leaning on the screen and looking down the block, a phone pressed to her ear.

I sat in the living room the rest of day, barely able to make it to the bathroom or to the kitchen for something to eat. My legs felt like they were made of rubber, so I sat on the corduroy sofa, biting my nails and counting flowers in the wallpaper. Outside, cars were going by, honking and playing their boom-boom music, like nothing had happened. Once in a while I would hear the voices of children or the cry of a baby out on the sidewalk, but nobody came to the door or called me to let me know what was happening.

I couldn't bring myself to pass the stairs, either to the front door or to go up them. When I slept—which wasn't much—it was on the sofa. I didn't have Johnquell's family's phone number, as I said, and after a certain hour I didn't dare go next door; Sherman Park isn't safe for a woman alone at night anymore.

I didn't see anyone from Johnquell's house for a couple of days. I left a message on Frances's machine to tell her I wasn't feeling well and wasn't coming to church. I spent every moment on pins and needles, waiting, so when the doorbell finally rang, on Monday afternoon, I nearly jumped out of my skin. By then I had thrown a towel from the powder room over the stair runner where the blood was, but I still hadn't been upstairs. I was wearing the housecoat and underpants I had on on Saturday morning.

Mrs. Braxton was at the door. Her clothes were rumpled and she didn't look me in the eye when she said hello. She pretty much pushed her way in, pressing me aside with her broad shoulders—Johnquell's shoulders, I saw now. Her face only came alive when she saw the stairs. Her eyes stuck on the towel once she saw it.

"I'm sorry. I didn't know you were coming," I said, putting myself between her and sight of the towel.

"I came to see it," she said. She put her heavy hand on my shoulder and moved me aside. The bookcase, actually, was wedged head down between the foot of the stairs and the foyer wall where the paramedics had left it, with some of the remaining books spilled out into a corner of the tile floor. Over the past few days, every once in a while, a book fell off, making me jump and sending a dose of bile up into my throat. Mrs. Braxton laid a hand on the bookcase and looked up the length of the stairs, then slid down to the bottom step like a pile of rags. She put her other hand on the towel and drew it up a little, clutching it like a handkerchief. It was clear she had been crying for a long time but a dry, catching sound came from her throat, the kind of sound someone makes when they're all tapped out. She looked thinner and her close-cropped hair was grayer than I remember.

"How's Johnquell doing?" I asked her after she sat there a moment on my stairs. "Is he feeling any better?"

Mrs. Braxton looked me in the face for the first time since she arrived on my doorstep, and it was like it took her a minute to realize where she was and who I am.

"His neck is broken," she said quietly. "He won't walk. We don't know yet what all will happen to him. The doctors say we'll have to wait and see." By the end of this short speech, her voice had changed. I remembered the sound from making the phone calls when Walt died. Like there wasn't any real feeling left in it; you're just getting it done, telling people.

I tried to think what people did to try to make me feel better.

"Can I make you some tea?" I asked.

Mrs. Braxton just nodded and stood up, wobbling a bit. She put her hand on the wall to steady herself and knocked into the hall mirror. "Which way?" she asked.

I motioned to her to follow me through the living room and I noticed as I passed that there was a sharp rectangle of dust outlining the place on the tan carpet where the bookcase had been.

My hands shook as I filled the kettle and put it on the stove with a horrible crash, but Mrs. Braxton didn't seem to notice. It took two turns of the knob to get the stove to light. I brought out the box of tea bags, two mugs, and two spoons, and set them on the table. Mrs. Braxton had her eyes on the door to the backyard.

"You just never know," she said. "You just never know."

"Never know what?" I asked, as I stood between the stove and table, shaking. I felt like one of those little spring rabbits in the yard, when you open the door to take out the trash and it's there in the grass, twitching its little nose and trying to figure out which way is the best way to run. As if I would ever hurt a little thing like that. It's funny, the way they can't tell somebody dangerous from somebody safe.

Mrs. Braxton answered my question, startling me. "You just never know when and where and why God is going to do what He is going to do. Especially the why."

"I don't think God had anything to do with it," I told her and she turned away from the door to look at me. The kettle whistled and I was glad to escape her stare by getting the water. Even holding the kettle with both hands, I still managed to slosh water all over the table.

"Oh dear," I said and mopped up the mess with a tea towel. It was one embroidered by Frances, with stars and stripes in red, white, and blue. Not a proper flag, just a hint of it. I wouldn't have taken the towel, even as a gift from Frances, and be wiping the table with it if it had the proper flag on it.

"What do you mean?"

"What?" I had lost track of what I had said.

"What do you mean, God didn't have anything to do with it?" She was looking right at me now.

"He just fell down the stairs and hurt himself. Why would God have anything to do with that?"

"God has something to do with every little thing. Like Jesus said, 'Are not two sparrows sold for a penny? And not one of them shall fall on the ground without your Father.' The sparrows, you, me, Johnquell. Every little thing." Mrs. Braxton stared again at the back door. If her gaze was an electric drill, there would have been a hole the size of Kansas in that door. In spite of her gospel-quoting, she looked angry, at me, at God, maybe both. Her jaw was set tight.

"Your tea is ready. You want sugar?"

Mrs. Braxton pulled her mug closer to her, but she left it on the table. I stirred a couple of teaspoons of sugar into my tea and brought it to my mouth. It was still too hot so I set it right back down.

"What do the doctors say?"

"He's a fighter, that's what they say. They say he's going to be in there a while. They got to keep his lungs clear for him because he isn't getting the stuff, the uh, mucus, out himself. His lungs are weak. But he's a fighter. He's a fighter." This last bit seemed mostly to herself as she picked up her tea and took a big drink, in spite of the heat. Walt was like that. We used to call him "Asbestos Mouth" because he could practically drink boiling water right out of the pot. Me, I'm thin skinned. I have to take my time, let things cool.

I was beginning to wonder why she was here. I mean, what did she expect me to do? I asked, "Is there something I can do for you, Mrs. Braxton?"

"It's Tibbetts," she said, "not Braxton. Johnquell's dad, he passed on before we could get married. He got caught up in the life, you know."

She looked at me like I was supposed to know what life she meant. I could guess but I must have shaken my head because she said, "Drugs. He was doing a little dealing 'cause he couldn't find a job. When I figured out I was pregnant I told him no baby of mine was going to get raised the child of a drug dealer. So he was fixing to get out, but I guess the guy above him felt different about the situation."

"He killed him?" I asked.

"That's what I'm saying," she said. She put her broad hand over her mouth, like she was wiping away something else she wanted to say. "So it's Tibbetts, my dad's name."

"Excuse me," I said. "Mrs. Tibbetts."

"Anyway, call me Gloria." For the first time, she softened a little. "We're neighbors, right? And now I realize I don't know your name."

Here she was sitting in my kitchen, drinking out of my cups, and she didn't know my name. "I'm Mrs. Czernicki. Margaret. My husband's name was Walter."

"Good to know," she said. "Funny, init, the way it takes something like this to get us talking. We been living right next door to each other for, what, five years and I didn't even know your name. That's a shame, a real shame." She resettled herself in the white spindle-back chair and for a moment, the cloud over her face lifted, like she was glad to have something else to talk about besides what might happen to her boy. "People don't know each other now. Not like they used to. If you never asked Johnquell to come over to help around the house, I might never known your name. And what if you needed something more serious? What if you needed help?"

"Oh, I don't know about that. I've got the girls. They live over in West Allis, just over the line. They look in on me. I'm fine. I'll be fine." I gave her a little smile while I straightened out the yellow flowered tablecloth on my little round breakfast table. I don't know why I still call it that, since I only ever eat here, not in the dining room anymore. It is the dining table now.

Mrs. Tibbetts—Gloria—was looking at me again. I think she was shaking her head a little bit, but so slightly it was almost hard to tell.

"What can I do for you?" I asked again.

"It's in God's hands, Mrs. Czernicki. I'd be grateful if you prayed for him, though."

"Oh, I will. I have been," I said, although that last part was kind of a lie. I hadn't been praying, exactly, but it wasn't like I had been thinking about anything else.

"Good. Good," she said. Her lips tightened and I could see some tears welling up. She closed her eyes for a moment, blinking away those tears, and then she looked up at me with an idea. "Your church got a prayer list?"

I nodded.

"Put him on your list at church, then." She pressed into the table with her thick index finger. "That's what you can do."

I tried to imagine this, writing his name on one of the little prayer request forms at St. Sebastian's: Please pray for Johnquell Braxton, a black boy with a broken neck. Millie, who leads the Saturday morning prayer circle, is a fussy little bird. I can hear her squawking, "John-quell? What kind of name is that? Isn't that some kind of flower? Why would they name a boy after a flower?"

"It is such a shame," I said. "Seventeen." I shook my head.

"He's going to be OK, Mrs. Czernicki," Gloria said with a sudden fierceness. "Johnquell he's going to college. He already got into UW, on a football scholarship. But he's not just some athlete, you know, he's a writer, too. He writes real good stories. He wrote a paper this year on Malcolm X that won the history prize from the county library. First time any child from the city beat those little white girls from Pius." Her eyes had a glow to them, that look when someone's trying to make themselves believe something they know isn't true. "I told him he could play football as long as he keeps up his grades in everything else. I told him, 'Only a fool counts on football. It just takes one good whack to the knee and that'll be all over.'" Her voice trickled away.

I didn't know what to say about any of that. The boy wasn't going to be playing football now and I doubt UW was going to give away a scholarship seat at one of the state's best schools to a cripple boy from the city. Spencer didn't get into UW. He didn't have the grades, but he tried anyway because Walt always wanted him to. Spencer hid the rejection letter in the garage, none too well. Walt found it one evening a few weeks later behind his toolbox on the workbench. I think Spencer meant for him to find it when he was out of the house. I don't know.

Gloria broke the quiet. "I should be going. My boss has been trying to be understanding so I can be at the hospital, but she can't wait forever. I'm going to have to go put in a couple hours this afternoon yet, get things straightened out a little bit, and then go back to the hospital tonight. They got a cot in the room for me." I was relieved to see that she had pulled herself together.

She stood up, pushing away from the table with both hands, like it was an effort to stand. "Yep. Got to go get things straightened out." She picked up her mug and the spoon and put them in the sink like she lived here.

I followed Gloria as she walked through the kitchen and dining room, through the living room, past the empty space where the bookcase used to be, and into the foyer.

"Johneitha has been watching the other girls while I'm away all this time, but I worry about them here by themselves," she said. "Can I give them your phone number, to call if something comes up?"

I said, "Of course." I didn't know how I could be of any help to them, but I thought it would be rude to say no, given the circumstances. Gloria gave me her cell phone number, too.

Just before she left, she turned toward the stairs one more time and reached for the towel, but she stopped herself, her hand hovering a moment over the cloth. When she stood up straight, I could see that her mouth was twisted funny, half up, half down, like she didn't know whether to smile or frown.

"It wasn't my fault, you know," I said and right away wished I hadn't.

Gloria looked at me again like she was trying to remember who I was. There was a second where I thought I saw a flicker of anger and I took a quick step back, slipping for a second on the tile.

She put out a hand to steady me. Her grip was strong and she made sure I was looking her in the eye when she said, "Mrs. Czernicki, it's nobody's fault."

I felt a wave of relief then, for the first time in days. I wasn't sure if this was OK but I reached out and patted Gloria's shoulder a little as she went out. Without turning around, Gloria patted my hand right back. "God bless," she said.

"You too," I said. As I lifted my arm to turn the deadbolt, I could smell myself. I smelled sour, the way your sheets stink after you've spent the night sweating out a high fever. I checked my hair in the foyer mirror. It was a tangle from sleeping on the cramped couch. I realized then how I must have looked to Gloria, a wrinkly, sour old woman, with a rat's nest of hair.

I told myself that if I went upstairs to the shower, I could sit on the bed afterward and call the kids. I could even call Spencer, long distance. I deserved it after such a hard time. I put my hand on the banister and pulled myself up to the first step. I looked down at the towel and stepped as quickly as I could up that stair and then the next and then the next. I didn't slow down at the bend in the stairs, just kept pulling myself upward, upward until I was on the landing outside the bathroom. I pushed my back into the wall, catching my breath.

The shower was good. It felt good to get clean and to just stand there under the water and watch my thoughts go by. I always did my best thinking in the shower. Comes from all those years raising kids, I guess. The shower was the only place I truly got to be alone with my thoughts. Not too much to think about now. Just current events—and those don't bear much contemplation. The world is a big mess and there isn't a darn thing I can do about it but pray.

After I wiped down the shower, I put on a fresh housecoat and got under my comforter. I pulled the yellow phone over to the edge of the nightstand and checked the piece of paper where the kids' phone numbers are written down. I dialed Spencer.

"Hello?"

"Hi, Spencer. It's Mom. How are you?"

"Mom, I'm good. I'm good." He sounded distracted. I could hear the sound of the TV in the background.

"What have you been up to?" I asked him.

"Same old, same old," he said.

"Are you still working for UPS?"

"Yeah. They're doing some layoffs, though, so I don't know how long that's going to last."

"Well, I hope not, dear. It's tough to find a job these days."

"Yeah."

I couldn't think of anything else to say, but I wanted to keep him on the line a little while longer. "Has the weather been good?" I asked.

"It's been OK. I spend most of my time in the warehouse or here, so it's not like it matters all that much."

"You should get outside more, get some fresh air. Do they have parks there?"

"Of course, Mom. They have parks everywhere. Why?" He was laughing at me a little bit, quietly but I could tell. It was that laugh that young people do when they think an old person is being dumb.

"I was just thinking you should get out, go play football or something, like you used to. It'd be good for you."

"I'm forty-nine, Mom. I haven't played any football since high school. And anyway, I smashed my elbow up a few months ago, loading boxes in the customer pick-up area, so I don't think the Packers' recruiter is going to want me anymore." He laughed again, but this time I think it wasn't just at me. Something on the TV, maybe.

"I don't mean like that," I said. "It's just to play. You'll miss it when you're older."

"I'm already older," he said.

We talked for a couple minutes more and then he said he needed to go. When he hung up I thought about calling Mary or Nancy, but I didn't. I wouldn't be able to keep from telling them about the boy and they would want to come over, so I just lay there looking at the afternoon light on the ceiling. Not five minutes later the phone rang.

"Hello?" I said.

"Hi, Mrs. Czernicki." The girl's voice on the other end of the line said it like "chair-necky" so I knew it wasn't someone I knew. It was a black voice, anyway. "This is Johneitha, next door. My mom gave me your number. She's back at work and the girls want their cereal but we don't have any milk."

"And?" I said. Was she expecting me to go to the store for her?

"Well, I was wondering, do you have some that we can have?" Johneitha's voice was very formal for her age. "I'm sure Mama will pay you back."

"Well, I suppose so." I was so stunned by the idea of this child calling me for help that I couldn't actually remember if there was any milk in the fridge or not.

"OK. Thanks!" she said. "I'll be right over."

Sure enough, the doorbell was ringing before I could even bring myself to start down the stairs.

I opened the door to find Johneitha there, a tall, skinny girl of maybe fourteen or fifteen but with a serious look that made her seem older than her years.

"Hi," she said.

"Just a minute," I said, not opening the screen door. Maybe it was rude to leave her out on the porch, but here she was asking for food and I guess I was a little in shock. In all these years since the neighborhood turned over, not one of my neighbors has ever called me, or rung my doorbell unexpected, unless it was one of those boys going house to house after a snowstorm, offering to clear your walks.

In the kitchen I looked for a little container to put some milk in, something plastic that I wouldn't mind losing. I found a deli container and poured some milk into it from the half gallon I found in the fridge. Then I came to my senses and realized that that little bit of milk wasn't going to be enough for cereal for three girls. Kids eat a lot of dry cereal these days. Mary's kids can eat an entire box in one sitting, like it was an actual meal. I put the deli container in the fridge and carried the half gallon out to the front door instead.

"Here you are," I said, cracking open the screen door and handing the jug to Johneitha.

"Do you need it back?" Johneitha asked.

"No, that's alright," I said.

"Thanks!" she said, and turned down the steps and walked carefully around the lawn and back to her house.

I slept in my own bed that night, and it felt so good, I slept until 9:30 the next morning, until the phone rang again and woke me up.

"Mrs. Czernicki?" It was Gloria. This time I could tell.

"Huh? Hello?" My voice was hoarse and I could hardly make the sound come out.

"This is Gloria Tibbetts. I'm at the office. I had to go straight from your house yesterday afternoon to the office, then the hospital, and now back to the office again. So I was wondering if you could go next door and check on the girls. I would ask one of my brothers or my sister but they're all at work."

She was asking me to go check on her children? How would I know whether they needed anything?

"What do you want me to do?" I asked. I found my glasses and blinked my eyes until I could open them all the way. The sun seemed bright for this late in the summer.

"Just go see that they're OK. My mind's not much on home. I don't even know what food's there for them in the kitchen. So, could you check, please?"

"I, well, sure. Sure, I'll do that. But it'll be a few minutes. I just woke up."

"That's fine. I expect to come home for just a little while around five or six and their Aunt Bee-Bee might come by earlier. I think I told

Johneitha that already, but I don't know. I have to go, though. My boss
is letting me use her office phone for calls like this, but I don't want to
take too much time. So, it's OK?" she asked.

"Yeah," I said.

Gloria sighed and said, "Thanks, Mrs. Czernicki," before hanging
up.

I sat on the edge of the bed and tried to think what I had gotten
myself into. I didn't want to become the babysitter of these kids and I
certainly didn't want to be their meal ticket. I have to feed myself, pay
my property taxes, buy a new pair of shoes now and then. I didn't have
much from Walt's pension, but it was enough to take care of me. Still,
that family had had a hard few days and it wouldn't hurt to help out a
little, for a while.

I put on a pair of slacks and a blouse and combed my hair. I needed
a hair appointment.

It took me some time to get down the stairs and across the lawn.
The day was already hot and I was sweating a little bit when I got to the
Tibbettses' door. The door and trim were painted black, which must
have looked sharp against the Cream City brick back when the bungalow
was first built, but the brick hadn't been washed in years and the paint
was dusty, giving the whole house a gray cast. The youngest girl must
have seen me coming because she opened the door before I could knock.
She stood there looking at me for a minute.

"Hello," I said. "I'm Mrs. Czernicki from next door. Is Johneitha
here?"

The little girl nodded, held open the bent aluminum screen, and
waited until I was inside before letting it slam behind me and running
upstairs. "Neitha!" she yelled. "Neitha! The white lady here to see you!"

Their house and mine were laid out exactly the same, with the stairs
running up from the foyer and the living room on the right. For some
reason that made me shiver. Johneitha came down the stairs right away
and said hello. She was dressed in shorts and a T-shirt, like it was a
regular summer day, but I knew she wouldn't be going out.

"Your mother called. She wanted me to see if you girls were alright. Looks like it, doesn't it?"

Johneitha nodded but I could see the worry in her eyes.

"Did you hear something from the hospital? About Johnquell?"

"No," she answered. There was a little twitch of her lips that told me I had hit on the very thing she was thinking about.

"I'm sure he's going to be OK. Your mother's got the whole world praying for him, right?" Except me, I thought. I'd spent the last three days on the sofa or in bed, too afraid to move, and I hadn't called Millie yet about the prayer list.

Johneitha nodded again and looked down at her feet. It was close in the foyer and I could feel that their air-conditioning wasn't working or maybe they didn't have any.

"You want some lemonade?" Johneitha asked.

"That would be nice," I said.

"Come on," Johneitha said, motioning me to follow her to the kitchen. In the living room was the middle girl, stretched out on the sofa reading a book. The girl didn't even seem to notice us walking through the room.

The kitchen was done up in 1970s colors, with avocado appliances, olive countertops, and yellow tile. I didn't know anybody still had a color scheme like that. Johneitha got out a pitcher from the refrigerator and some ice cubes from the freezer. She poured me a big glass before pouring another one for herself and then calling out, "Johnraye! You want some lemonade?"

"No! Why you always interrupting me?" Johnraye yelled back from the living room.

Johneitha rolled her eyes while handing me my glass. "'Cause I got some manners, that's why—not like some people who make themselves a glass of something and don't offer anybody else none."

"Why do all of your names start with 'John'?" I had wanted to know this all along, but her calling out her sister's name gave me an opportunity to ask without it seeming strange.

"That was our granddaddy's name."

"Your mom's father?"

"Yeah. My mom was real proud of him 'cause he was like a civil rights hero. He marched with Father Groppi to stop the housing segregation. He was a Panther too." Johneitha turned to put the ice cubes and the pitcher away, so I don't think she saw me shudder. The Panthers caused a lot of trouble, for all of us.

I could hear the other girl upstairs singing to herself. I drank some of my lemonade and was surprised to find it was real, not from a powder. "Oh, that's good," I said.

"Yeah, my mom says it isn't worth it if it isn't real, so in the summertime we squeeze the lemons ourselves. Other folks use that mix."

I drank the lemonade in a few big gulps because I didn't know how long I should stay. I said, "Your mother asked me to come over here to check on you girls. Is there anything you need?"

A mound of dishes in the sink, including my now-empty jug of milk, had nearly reached the faucet. Besides that, things seemed under control.

Just then the little girl came into the kitchen. She looked about six or seven years old, with fat braids flopping over on either side of her head pinned with pink butterfly barrettes.

"What day is it?" the little girl asked Johneitha.

"It's Monday," said Johneitha.

"No, it ain't," the little girl said.

"It's Monday, Johnelle," Johneitha said again.

"It's not. It's Tuesday. It's chicken day. I know," Johnelle said, looking up at Johneitha with her little hands balled up on her hips.

"What's chicken day?" I asked Johneitha.

"My mom always makes chicken on Tuesdays. It's Nelly's favorite day of the week," Johneitha said to me. Then she turned to Johnelle and said, "Until Mama comes home, it's Monday, OK?"

Johnelle stuck out her tongue at Johneitha and ran back out of the room.

"I can make you chicken," I said. The words were out of my mouth before I could catch them. Johneitha's eyes lit up when I said it, though. She was a pretty girl when the worry was off her face.

"What kind of chicken does your mother make?" I asked.

"Fried, usually. Barbecue if she has time to set up the grill. Nelly can wait, though. We got food. You don't have to worry about us." She pulled her shoulders back and straightened up, like she had made up her mind to let me out of it. I could just say thanks for the lemonade and get out of there, tell Gloria they were fine, didn't need anything.

"Well, OK," I said. "Are you sure?" Fourteen was young to be running a household, even for a couple of days.

"Yeah, we'll be OK." Johneitha took my empty glass from my hand. I had been holding it so tightly my knuckles were aching from the cold. She walked me to the door.

"Well, you have my number," I said.

"Yeah," Johneitha said, nodding as she shut the door behind me.

At home I sat in the kitchen, thinking over the events of the past few days, until the growling in my stomach brought me back to today. I fried myself an egg and had a slice of toast, though by now it was lunch time. In a few hours Frances would be coming to pick me up for the four o'clock bingo. That gave me an idea.

I dialed Frances's number on the kitchen phone while I pulled out my *Joy of Cooking*. Frances answered with her typical "Yell-o?" I think she thought that was cute.

"Frances, I need your help."

"Margie?"

"Yeah. Frances, I need your help to make some fried chicken."

"What? No, we're going to bingo and then we're going to Webb's, remember? What, are you going senile on me? It's Tuesday." She was laughing at me like I was a fool.

"No, Frances, we can't go to bingo tonight. I need to make some chicken, only, I don't know how. Walt never liked his chicken fried, so I don't know how."

"He always was an odd duck. Who doesn't like fried chicken?" Frances said. "Are you OK?"

"Yes, why?"

"You sound, I don't know, like you've been hitting the cough syrup. What's going on?"

"You know that black family that lives next door to me?"

"Hmm. Let's see. Which one?" she said. She was such an irritating smart aleck sometimes.

"The one to the south, in the yellow brick house like mine. But that's not important. Their boy, Johnquell . . ."

"Jonquil? Isn't that some kind of flower?"

"No, it's the boy's name. Johnquell," I said, stressing the second syllable. "He fell down my stairs while moving a bookcase and now he's in the hospital and his sisters need me to make them some chicken." I knew I wasn't making any sense, or enough sense anyway to get Frances to understand. "Just come pick me up, OK? We need to go to Piggly Wiggly."

"But Senior Discount Day is on Wednesday. It can wait 'til Wednesday, can't it?"

"No, Frances. Chicken Day is today. How soon can you be here?"

Frances was my best friend, although usually I only saw her on Tuesdays and Sundays. She was my age, but she had held onto her energy somehow and moved faster, got involved in things. She liked to get out of the house, so I knew she would be willing to come over and help me out. Not without a fuss first, of course, but she'd do it.

"Fine. I'll be there in a half hour but you better be done with this clowning around in time for the four o'clock Early Bird." She grumbled, but I could tell she was glad to be needed.

I made out the list of ingredients for pan-fried chicken and gravy, and added on some frozen corn, a gallon of milk, and some potatoes for mashing. Frances was at my house at a quarter to one and we were at the cash register ringing up a half hour later.

"Geez, $31.73! Who are these kids to you that you're spending that kind of money on their dinner?" I had thrown in a pound cake and some strawberries at the last minute to make the girls some dessert. I looked at Frances. She was leaning in over the conveyor. Behind her glasses, her eyes were working up the numbers on the cash register screen, double-checking the total.

What did she care what I was spending? I thought to myself, but I didn't want to get into it with her right there at the register with the check-out girl listening in.

I had Frances pull the car up at the Tibbettses' walkway and we carried the groceries up to the door. Before I rang the bell I said to Frances, "Act natural, OK?"

Frances pulled back like I had tried to hit her. "What's that supposed to mean?"

"Just be . . . they're people, you know?" I wasn't sure exactly what I was trying to tell her, but I knew I couldn't deal with her—I don't know what to call it—Frances-ness right now. I pressed the bell.

The littlest one answered the door this time, too. Johnelle.

"Hi, Johnelle," I said.

She held the screen door open for us, pressing her little hand into the mesh and concentrating on the effort. When we were inside she pointed to the bag in my arms and said, "Is that chicken?" Her face lit up like she had just guessed the right answer on *Family Feud*.

Frances rolled her eyes and I elbowed her in the ribs.

"It is. This is my friend, Mrs. Clark, and she's going to help me make you girls some dinner. What do you think about that?"

Johnelle clapped and said, "Good idea!" Then she turned and shouted up the stairs to Johneitha. "Neitha! Come down here. Mrs. Chair-necky going to make us some chicken."

Johneitha was surprised to see us. "It's OK, Mrs. Czernicki. You didn't have to go to the store for us. My auntie just called and said she's coming by this afternoon."

"For cryin' out loud," Frances said under her breath. I got her in the ribs with another jab of my elbow.

"Well, fried chicken keeps, doesn't it? We'll just make it and then if you don't want it for dinner you can just put it in the refrigerator for later. Or your mom might want some when she comes home." Even at this late moment I guess I was still trying to talk myself into this, trying to generate some momentum to pull Frances along, too.

Neitha gave me a little smile and went to the kitchen ahead of us and began taking out some pans. Besides giving me orders, Frances kept quiet. That sure wasn't acting natural for her, but I appreciated her silence given the alternatives. With Frances telling me what to do and Neitha anticipating my need for the jug of vegetable oil or a paper towel or what have you before I could even say anything, it turned out to be much easier to make fried chicken than I thought.

Johnelle swept in and out of the room, making sure we were doing it right. When I could catch her for a minute, I put her to work, washing the strawberries and the like. We didn't say much, just listened to Johnelle singing to herself and making the potatoes talk like the characters in some cartoon before she peeled them. Johnraye stood at the kitchen's swinging door once in a while, not speaking, just watching. She kept her arms crossed over her purple sundress as she stood, the book she had been reading pushed up into her armpit. Johnraye reminded me of one of those British soldiers outside Buckingham Palace, the ones who never smile.

A little after three o'clock, when we were just getting done with the cooking, the doorbell rang. Johnraye went to answer it. I guessed it was the aunt, Bee-Bee. She and Johnraye were having a conversation in the living room but I couldn't make out what they were saying. I heard Bee-Bee groan.

Bee-Bee came into the room. She was tall, like Gloria, but with a more slender build. Her straight black hair was pulled into a pony tail. She had on a uniform kind of like a cop's except brown. I tried to read the gold badge on her chest but I couldn't make it out.

"How you doing," Bee-Bee said to me and Frances. "Girls, why you got on these nice ladies to make you some chicken when you know I was coming to take you out to eat?"

Neitha and Johnelle just looked up at Bee-Bee and didn't say anything.

"I told you," said Johnraye, slapping her hand on her thigh and going back to the living room.

"It's alright," I said, wiping my hands on the dish towel I had on my shoulder. "No harm done." I looked at Frances, whose pink-lipsticked mouth was stretched out into one of those straight-line smiles that isn't really a smile.

"Yeah, it's Chicken Day," said Johnelle into the plastic tub of Cool Whip she had been holding for the past several minutes while trying to talk me into giving her an early dessert. The temperature in the room had dropped a few degrees since Bee-Bee had stepped in.

"I'm Margaret Czernicki," I said, extending my hand, which Bee-Bee shook so briefly it was like she was afraid it might bite her. "And this is my friend, Frances Clark." Again, the briefest of handshakes.

During this little exchange, Johnelle and Johneitha had started taking the food out to the dining room table. They just about had everything out there by the time Bee-Bee was done giving us her icy appraisal.

I said, "Well, there's plenty of food right here, in case you decide you don't want to go out." For a second, I wondered if she might ask us to sit down but who were Frances and me, anyway? Just strangers in her sister's house.

Frances pulled on my sleeve. "Margie, we better be going if we're still going to make our four o'clock appointment, right?" She looked at me with eyebrows raised and mouth tight. Still ordering me around. I looked at Neitha and Johnelle, in the doorway watching. They looked like I felt, disappointed, maybe even intruded upon somehow.

Johnelle said, "No," and started jumping up and down, yelling, "Stay! Stay! Stay!"

I went to her and said, "Johnelle, you enjoy your dinner, OK? And maybe I can come back tomorrow and see how you liked it. Alright?"

Johnelle didn't answer but she stopped the jumping and yelling at least. I got my pocketbook from the counter and Frances got hers and Bee-Bee began to walk us to the front door.

"Thank you for stopping by," Bee-Bee said.

Out on the street, getting back into Frances's car, Frances asked me, "What was all that about?"

"What was what about?" I said, lowering myself into the seat of her Buick.

"What's with her?"

"You mean Bee-Bee?"

"Yeah. Here we are spending our whole afternoon making her family a nice dinner and she treats us like we're the kitchen help, wanting to sit down to eat at the table." She snorted.

"It wasn't that big of a deal," I said. But Frances just went on the whole ride to the bingo hall about the nerve of some people and we were so nice when we didn't even owe them anything and what about the middle girl with her haughty stare until finally I had to say, "Frances, it's a hard time for them. You weren't exactly Emily Post when Chester was in the hospital, remember?"

"I don't remember," Frances said, but she shut up then. A couple of times, when we were stopped at stoplights, I felt her staring at me. I didn't turn to look, though.

We didn't win at bingo. We ate our Salisbury steak at Webb's in near silence. I was relieved when Frances let me out in front of my house.

"See you Sunday," I said, squinting to see into the window against the pink glare of the sunset.

Frances pursed her lips and nodded. She lifted the fingers of her right hand off the steering wheel in a little wave and then drove off.

I had left so early in the afternoon that I didn't think to leave the lights on for when I got back. When I hit the switch in the dark foyer I was surprised to see the towel still on the stairs. It finally occurred to me that the carpet would have to be pulled up and replaced. The blood was never going to come out. Maybe it even soaked into the wood below. The thought, the forever-ness of it, made me cry tears that stung my tired eyes. I sat down on the stairs. I cried for those girls, and for Gloria, and for Johnquell. I cried because things between me and Frances used to be different. We used to be the same. I cried because Bee-Bee was so angry and I thought that in some way it must be my fault.

I sat there a while, until the doorbell buzzed, startling me.

"Who is it?" I called through the door. I got up and looked out through the peephole but I didn't see anybody. Then I heard the voices of a couple kids screeching and giggling, like they were playing Cowboys and Indians on my lawn. I opened the door quickly but there was no one there. On the stoop, though, was a brown paper grocery bag. It was folded down at the top and I could see the Piggly Wiggly pig's fat face smiling on the front.

I picked the bag up. In black marker at the top it said "To Mrs. Chernicky" in a child's big, uneven print. I looked around again, toward the Tibbettses' house, but I was the only one out there.

The phone rang so I locked the door and picked up the phone in the living room. I almost didn't believe it when I heard Bee-Bee's voice on the line.

"Gloria told me I should call," she said, in a voice just as gruff as that afternoon. "Johnquell, he passed. The doctors told Gloria it was nearly time and she got us all down to the hospital this evening. We're all here with her and she says call Mrs. Czernicki and ask will she keep an ear out for the girls. The girls don't know anything yet. I'll be bringing Gloria home in a little while. It won't be but an hour or two."

I couldn't speak. I just held onto the phone. I could hear Bee-Bee rustling around with something on the other end of the line. "Mrs. Czernicki," she finally said.

"Yes?"

"You can call us if there's any problem. OK?"

"Yes. Yes, it's fine," I said and hung up.

I couldn't think. Johnquell was so healthy and strong. Here in my house he had lifted that bookcase like it was nothing. When I tried to puzzle through how he could be dead, I would only get so far before my thoughts flipped around in my mind like a caught fish on the floor of a boat. It didn't make any sense. I stood there in a daze for a minute, staring into the foyer where he had been, until I felt the weight of the paper bag straining my shoulder. I had forgotten I was still holding it.

I brought the bag into the kitchen and opened it on the breakfast table. Inside was a doubled-up paper plate with foil over it and a clear plastic container with a piece of strawberry pound cake in it. On the plate the girls had arranged two pieces of chicken, some corn, and some potatoes and gravy. I reached for the phone to call Frances, to tell her about Johnquell and maybe mention that the girls had brought us dinner after all, that they were grateful, but then I remembered her face in the car, and the way she waved with just her fingers, not even her whole hand, before driving off.

Instead, I put the food in the fridge for later and went next door to tell the girls thank you.

Fragging

This dude he don't know the first thing about U.S. history but he's up there at the front of the class like Moses, coming down the mountain to deliver the truth to us wandering Israelites. Or one particular Israelite, anyhow.

"Mr. Braxton," dude says to me. He's sitting on the edge of Mrs. Charles's desk and he's got my Long Binh paper in his hand, holding it close to his chest and leaning back a little, like he's keeping it for himself. He's always talking like we're at the bank and he's about to give me a big loan or something. *Mr. Braxton.*

Dude's funny-looking too, with these wrinkles on the sides of his mouth so deep they look like he's got another mouth on each side, with lips that move when he talks. His real mouth is full of big old fake teeth that are super white and can't hardly fit in his face. Every day he's got on one of these polo shirts—not a Polo polo, but some kind of Nolo fake he probably got from Kohl's—tucked into his khakis.

He rolls up my paper and unrolls it, then taps it with his finger. His eyes got a spark to them. "I was really interested to see your comments about life on the bases in Vietnam during the war, Mr. Braxton. Were you there?"

"I ain't even gonna answer that," I tell him. He thinks he's being real funny. From the minute he got here on Wednesday, he's been bragging on being a Vietnam vet. *Was I there?*

"I'm just asking because you make some pretty serious allegations against the white soldiers at Long Binh and I'm wondering what your evidence is." I feel the eyes of the class on me, 'cause I'm right in the middle of the room. "Evidence, Mr. Braxton, is the foundation of history. Of truth."

I didn't write that paper for him. I wrote it for Mrs. Charles. She knows why I wrote it, too. But she's gone right now, leukemia or something, they don't know what all yet. Mrs. Charles she was getting skinnier and paler for a long time. She just kept saying she's OK but then on Tuesday Taquan says she passed out in first hour and they took her to the hospital. She's going to be out for a while and now our history class got to put up with Mr. Honorable Discharge for who knows how long. If I'da known this dude was going to read my paper instead of Mrs. Charles, I woulda kept it to myself. I woulda took the zero. Two weeks until graduation, I ain't trying to waste time on a man who don't know nothing about black history.

When Mrs. Charles assigned this paper, she said pick any topic that connects the 1960s to now. I knew right away what I wanted to write about. I remember my mom she told me she heard some idiot on the TV talking about the Obamas giving each other some dap after one of his campaign speeches and how it was some kind of "terrorist fist bump." I looked up the clip on the Internet and it was as bad as Moms said. So I wrote my paper on the history of the dap and how black soldiers used it to show their pride during the Vietnam War. But then I got all caught up in reading about the 1968 Long Binh Jail riots and so the paper turned out mostly about that. I get that way when I'm reading history. I want to know how come this thing happened and who did what and then I don't get too far down that road before I want to find out about something else. "An inquisitive mind," my eighth-grade teacher at Grand Avenue School called it. I remember that from my report card because I got all As and Moms stuck it on the fridge.

"When Ms. Charles be back?" I ask instead of answering him. I can tell he's the kind of white dude gets all worked up when black people start talking street. Just knowing that he's gonna be tripping on it makes me want to do it more.

"'When *is Mrs.* Charles *coming* back?'" dude says. "Mrs. Charles is out indefinitely—that means we don't know when she's coming back," he says, looking at me like I'm the only one in the class who might not know what "indefinitely" means but I do. "We will all hope for Mrs. Charles's speedy recovery, but in the meantime you're going to work with me. Your principal requested a substitute who could stay through the end of the year and here I am. I might have mentioned when I arrived that I majored in U.S. history when I was at UNC–Chapel Hill. And lucky for Mr. Braxton," he says, now looking dead at me, "I served three years in Vietnam, 1968 to 1971, with the Military Police 721st Battalion. And it seems like you know where the MP 721st was stationed in 1968, Mr. Braxton."

I can't help it, but my mouth falls open. I try to shut it real quick, before any of the other kids see. Mr. Honorable Discharge sees it, though, and I can tell in his eyes he's trying not to laugh. Dude is like pure evil.

"Why don't you read us your paper, Mr. Braxton?" he says. It ain't a question. He hands me the paper.

I can feel the eyes of the other kids all over me again. Sometimes being the only black guy in Advanced U.S. History makes me feel like some kind of animal in the zoo everybody's staring at. It's 2013, but it's still segregated around here. Moms says it's getting better, but she still plays this game in her head when somebody new sends her an e-mail or calls at the county office where she works: "Tell me your address and I'll tell you your color." She wins most of the time.

I been at this school for three years, part of the voluntary integration program between Whitefish Bay ("Whitefolks Bay," we call it) and Milwaukee. They seen me every day for three years, but I'm still on the outside. The kids in this class in particular they hate me because Mrs. Charles and I got a bond and it ain't just about the skin color. She understands me. No teacher ever got me the way Mrs. Charles does. She knows I'ma be somebody. And now she's gone and this fool is here, trying me. *"Why don't you read us your paper, Mr. Braxton?"*

I'll read it alright, maybe teach them something they don't know. There's a lot things they don't know, so I can pretty much start anywhere.

Johnquell X. Braxton
June 6, 2013
Advanced U.S. History
Mrs. Charles
4th Hour

Brothers in the Struggle:
Long Binh Jail and the History of the Dap

When the first African American President of the United States of America Barack Obama, and his wife First Lady Michelle Obama, celebrated a speech he gave on June 3, 2008 they celebrated by dapping. A reporter on Fox news called this traditional greeting with the hands, a "terrorist fist jab" and then black Americans knew it was high time to educate everybody about dap and it's place in the black culture.

Some people say "dap" stands for "Dignity and Pride" but most researchers think it's just the word "tap" changed to make it a little bit different. The "Dignity and Pride" connection probably came later. Since the dap started with black soldiers in Vietnam, other researchers think it might be coming from the Vietnamese word "dep," which means "beautiful." That doesn't seem likely though since "dep" and "dap" sound different and no one can explain why Vietnamese people would think a black symbol would be beautiful.

To give someone dap, you make a fist and they make a fist and you bump the knuckles together. From there, you can take it a lot of ways, adding on hand shakes, high fives, finger or thumb locks, taps, waves, snaps, chest bumps, pound hugs, and other moves to make the greeting longer. Friends can have particular daps that only they know and different groups can have daps that show they belong.

How did the dap start? Most researchers say that the dap started among the black prisoners in the Long Binh Stockade, also known as "Long Binh Jail" or "LBJ" for short, to make fun of President Lyndon B. Johnson who a lot of people blamed for the war. Like in America today, there was a lot of racism against African Americans in Vietnam. Racial discrimination against black soldiers included worse punishment for breaking rules or committing crimes than what the white soldiers got for doing the same thing. Sometimes the discrimination was basic things like not having black hair care products in the PX or black music on the jukeboxes in the soldiers clubs or black entertainers in the USO tours. But lots of times it was more serious, like a white officer calling a black soldier "boy" or worse, or giving the black soldiers the most dangerous duty or the worst punishments.

Even though they were far away, the soldiers in Vietnam still got news from America, including news like the assassination of Dr. Martin Luther King Jr. in 1968. Dr. King gave a speech against the war in Vietnam that made some government leaders angry and many African Americans thought the U.S. government had him assassinated to keep him from giving more speeches against the war. Many African American soldiers got involved in the Black Power or Black Pride movements after that. Dapping was a way the soldiers could show there solidarity with there black brothers in Vietnam and back at home. They invented dap greetings that took up to 5 minutes to do. They also made Black Power flags and other symbols to wear on their uniforms and wrote Black Power sayings on their helmets.

Long Binh Stockade was part of the massive Long Binh military base in Vietnam. It was so big it was like it's own city and it had everything: restaurants, a post office, a movie theater, a bowling alley, dentist offices, bars, and even a college so soldiers could take classes. The jail was mainly for U.S. soldiers who had committed crimes or didn't follow the orders of their superior officers.

Just like in American jails, there were more black inmates than white inmates, and most of the guards were white. Nearly every day, the guards humiliated the prisoners using racist language and disrespectful punishments. African American prisoners complained that white prisoners got better treatment, food, and priviliges. More black prisoners than white prisoners spent time in "Silver City" the solitary confinement block made of metal shipping containers where the temperature sometimes got to 110F degrees inside. What made the situation worse was that LBJ was only built to hold around 270 prisoners but there were over 700 in it in the summer of 1968. The final straw came when strip searches of prisoners were ordered with the excuse that the guards were looking for drugs, which were a big problem in LBJ and pretty much everywhere in Vietnam during the war. The black prisoners felt it was time to fight for there dignity and freedom.

On August29 1968 a fight broke out between black and white prisoners. When a guard came to break up the fight, a black prisoner took his keys and began opening the doors of the other prisoner's cells. Soon there were hundreds of prisoners running through LBJ, setting buildings on fire and trying to break out. The African American prisoners expressed their pride by taking off their uniforms and putting on homemade dashikis instead and shouting Black Power slogans. Four prisoners escaped and one white prisoner was killed by the other inmates.

The Military Police 721st Battalion (an elite police force that was just about 100% white at the time) was called in to put down the riot. They charged the prisoners with there bayonets and tear gas, pushing the rioters back into the prison yard. Dozens of prisoners were injured.

The MPs separated the inmates who were not participating in the riot and put them at one end of the yard, under armed guard. The ones who were not participating were given the chance to be taken away to another location if they wanted. This isn't going to surprise you but all of the prisoners who got to leave were white. The ones that got left in the chaos were black with a few Puerto Ricans in the mix.

The brothers continued this standoff for three weeks but the police just waited them out, letting them go hungry and thirsty in the yard, until on Sept. 21st the last 13 fighters surrendered. Although black and white prisoners were involved in the fight that began the riot, again, it probably isn't going to surprise you that only black prisoners were charged with crimes that happened during the riot.

In conclusion, the African American greeting, the dap, came about in a time and place where Black Pride was necessary for survival. It was a way for brothers to show solidarity in a situation where they faced the same kinds of discrimination, bad treatment and violence that they experienced back in the States.

I hear a bunch of kids shift in their seats when I get done.

"It's a pretty good paper," Mr. Discharge says. He smiling at me and I can't tell if he's for real or not. "I'm amazed that you were able to unearth this lost bit of history. Seems like hardly anyone knows anymore—or cares—what happened at Long Binh." Dude bites his lip with those white horse teeth and squints one eye, like he's trying to figure something out. He reaches out his hand for the paper, so I give it to him. "Since you brought it up, I'll take another look at this and tomorrow I'll try to clear up some misconceptions. It's important for us to remember, but it's essential that we remember correctly."

"What do you mean, 'misconceptions'?" I ask.

"'Misconception'? It means 'misunderstanding.'"

I half stand up and smack my knee on the underside of my desk, making my pen roll off onto the floor. Nobody picks it up. The other kids just watch. The room has that hot feeling a place gets when people are holding their breath and kind of hoping something goes down.

"I know what the word means," I say. "I ain't stupid. What I'm asking is, why you gonna pull my paper apart in front of the whole class and not anybody else's?"

Dude straightens up in front of the desk. He crosses his arms on his chest and says, "Because as far as I can see, nobody else put their particular racial spin on the historical moment they wrote about."

"You know, what?" I start to say, but I don't know where to go with it. There's just so much to say. I stand up and get my pen off the floor. Then I think of what it is I mean and I sit down. "It's like this, history don't happen to just one person. It happens to all of us all at the same time. Like this moment right here," I say. "If something happened in this room right now worth putting in the history books, every one of us would see it different. Right?"

I look around at the other desks. "Am I right?" Most of the kids are acting like all of a sudden they aren't interested. On my left, Kyle is sneaking his ear bud from his iPod into his ear and on the right that Hayley girl looks like she's finally getting around to reading the Statue of Liberty poster Mrs. Charles put up on the wall on the first day of class.

Half of Mr. Discharge's weird mouth turns up, just one corner, and he shakes his head at me. "Having an opinion about what happened is materially different from the researched, documented, established truth, Mr. Braxton. We all have opinions."

He turns away from me to write the homework on the board. He's talking about the assignment but I can't take anymore of him, so I watch the clock on the wall click through the last five minutes of class.

When the bell rings I pick up my book bag and move for the door, but the sub puts his hand on my chest and says, "Hang on. I'm curious about something." He's smiling but it's that kind of pleased with himself smile that don't mean nothing. I can feel other students rushing past

me, like a dam just broke. "Tell me, how come you write in regular
English but you talk like some kind of gangster rapper?"

I look down at him—dude must be three inches shorter than me—
and push his hand off me. He's gotta see the flash in my eyes, but he
just goes on anyway.

"Now, don't be angry. This is an honest question. I can see you're a
smart kid. If you know how to talk correctly, why don't you?"

He's so close his drugstore aftershave is getting into my nose and I
can count the gray hairs on his head. I got the strap of my book bag over
my shoulder and I squeeze it with both hands to keep from smacking
him.

"I . . . am . . . going . . . to . . . class," I say, slowing the words way
down like he's deaf and needs to read my lips. "That English, right?" I
ask when I push past him.

In the hallway it's hot, even though the school got air and half the
students are already out of the halls and in their next class. I lied to Mr.
Discharge. I got lunch this period, not class, but I don't feel hungry
anymore. I go to the main office instead to ask Miss Snopes a question.
Miss Snopes is the secretary and a friend of my mom's from church.

"Hey, Johnquell," Miss Snopes says when I walk in. She's got a big
stack of papers on her desk and she's folding them and putting them in
a box that used to have copy paper in it. "How you doing?"

"Aiight," I tell her. "How about you?"

"Oh, busy, getting the programs ready for the senior recital." Miss
Snopes is always busy and she can be doing like three things at once
while she's still keeping up a conversation with whoever.

"Where Mrs. Charles at?" I ask. I rub the edge of the dark wood
counter with my palm. I got a superstition that touching it makes you
invincible, 'cause it's so old.

Miss Snopes stops folding to push a piece of her straightened hair
out of her eyes and looks at me serious. "She's at home now, Johnquell,
waiting on the test results. I'm praying for her. I'm sure she would

appreciate a note from you. If you bring it in I'll get it to her for you."
Miss Snopes knows Mrs. Charles is my favorite teacher.

"Thank you," I say. "I'ma do that." Before I leave the office the
phone's already rung twice and Miss Snopes is on to the next thing.

In the cafeteria I find Taquan, which isn't hard. He's one of the
maybe 20 of us here in a school of 1,200. Integration my ass. We don't
amount to more than a little sprinkle of pepper in a whole pile of salt.
Just enough to add a little color. Not enough to change the flavor.
Taquan and I are both from the city but not the same neighborhood so
on the outside we probably wouldn't even be friends. Here, though, we're
the only two black guys made it this far, the only two senior guys left.

"Hey, Robeson, what up?" Taquan calls me "Robeson" as a kind
of joke. Mrs. Charles taught us about Paul Robeson when we were
sophomores, the same year I went out for the JV football team and got
put on varsity instead, my first year at Whitefolks. "Our football
scholar," Mrs. Charles calls me.

"Not much, Taco," I say. I call him Taco 'cause he's half Hispanic.
He tries to tell me all the time he's half Puerto Rican/half black and
that's different from Mexican, but he's a hundred percent black as far as
the people around here concerned. Still, he's a lot lighter than me, and
shorter and skinnier too, and got these pale brown eyes like nobody I've
ever seen. "You want to skip out and go see Mrs. Charles?"

Taco thinks about it for all of half a second and then he says, "Let's
go." He shoves the end of his hamburger into his mouth and dumps his
tray. He waves bye to Rhonda, Angelique, and Tiana—aka the rest of
the black senior class—and says bye to Rhonda in particular with some
kinda wink he must think is cute. He's been cupcaking with Rhonda
since forever, but they never gone out.

We done this before so we know that the best place to get out
without nobody seeing is the doors behind the pool. It's only Jenny
Portillo in the pool, doing laps on her lunch hour 'cause she's going out
for the Olympic team next year. We gotta hear about that like every five

minutes on the announcements. She's always going around school selling candy bars to raise money for her trip to the tryouts. It sure doesn't look like she eats any of them herself, though, she's so skinny. The smell of chlorine is strong and Taco sneezes, but Jenny doesn't seem to hear. We just push through the doors and out onto the muddy field behind the school.

"What your mom gonna say when she find out you skipped?" Taco asks me.

"Nothing. She'll put some more chores on me, but she knows I'm gonna graduate and that's what matters to her."

"Huh," Taco says. I know it's always worse on him. Whether he's getting his diploma is still a question, but the belt ain't. He's gonna get that. Taco isn't the sharpest crayon in the box, but he's OK.

We know where Mrs. Charles lives because the summer after junior year she had me and Taco come over to paint her shutters. I think she wanted to keep an eye on us, too. She's like that, watching out for the black students, especially the boys. She knows it's hard on us. She's been teaching there since 1972 or something and for most of those years it was all white—students and teachers. She was the only piece of pepper for a long time. Her and then Mr. Perry, the janitor.

"What you think college gonna be like?" Taco asks. My mom put me in a "college readiness" program in Madison for a couple weeks last summer, so I kind of know. For me, college is a reality, but Taco he's still just daydreaming. He didn't even put in any applications and now here we are just two weeks from graduation.

"Why? You all of a sudden planning to go?" I ask back.

"Yeah, I'ma go. I'ma take a year off, save up first." He sticks out his lower lip, like he's thinking.

"Lot of people say that but they don't end up in college." I don't say it but I bet he's remembering Tanay. She's real smart. She graduated from Whitefolks last year but now she's working at Target on the south side and got a baby.

I'm still thinking about her when a car comes up behind us. I hear the ping-ping of some little rocks in the gutter hitting the underside of the car as it slows down. Mrs. Charles's house is just two more doors down so we don't even have to talk about it, we just keep walking like we don't notice anything going on. There's the sound of a car door opening and then slamming shut.

"Hey, you there, young men." It's a cop. I can hear the voice of the dispatcher on his radio. We still don't turn around, just make a right into Mrs. Charles's yard. "Young men, you stop right there," the cop calls again.

We're halfway up Mrs. Charles's sidewalk and again Taco and I don't even have to ask. We both know we're in a good spot to turn around now so we do. We know the drill. "Yes, sir?" I say.

"What are you boys doing out of school?" the cop asks. He's a little tubby around the middle but he looks young, twenty-five maybe. He got his hands on his hips. He looks kind of ridiculous, like an angry mom out of a cartoon, but I notice he's keeping his fingers close to the handle of his gun so I don't laugh.

"Well, sir," I say. I'm giving him my straight-A voice. Maybe Mr. Discharge can't see how someone can have more than one voice—one for the street, one for home, one for the bullshit—but that's because he's an idiot. "Our teacher, Mrs. Charles, is sick and we need to get our homework back from her."

"Why doesn't she just bring it when she comes back to school?" He's chewing on the inside corner of his mouth, like he's trying to figure us out.

"No, sir. It's not like that. She's real sick. We don't know when she'll be back and we have a project we got to get done before graduation."

"Is that what she would say if we knocked on her door right now, young man?" the cop asks. He sounds just like they do on TV, like they all got some kind of script.

"Yes, sir," I say. Taco just nods.

"Well, let's go then," the cop says, pointing at the door with the hand that's not on his gun.

Taco just stands there when we get to the stoop so I reach over and ring the bell. I can smell Taco. He's sweating. This is why he and I can never be friends for real. He worries too much.

When Mrs. Charles comes to the door I can't say a word. She looks so small. I mean, she always looks small, but not like this. All wrapped up in a housecoat with her little house shoes on she looks tiny. And sick. Her skin's all ashy and her hair's wild.

"Why, boys . . . ," she starts but I frown and shake my head just a little bit and she stops and talks to the cop instead. "What can I do for you, officer?" she says.

"These boys say that they were coming from school to pick up their homework. Is that right?" Damn, he's dumb. Sometimes you just got to let these fools talk and they fill in all the blanks.

"Yes, of course," Mrs. Charles says. "This is Johnquell and this is Taquan. They're my students at the high school. Are they in trouble?" She gives the dumb cop a sweet old lady smile I ain't never seen her do before.

"Not yet, but we'll see," he says, taking out his little cop notebook. "Spell your names. You first." He looks at Taco.

"T-A-Q-U-A-N F-I-E-L-D-S," Taco spells out.

"Middle name?"

"Carrasquillo," Taco says and it's like another person is talking. A Spanish person.

The cop says, "Spell that," and Taco does.

The cop he takes my name, too, and our birthdays and addresses and goes back to the squad to run us through the computer. Meantime, Mrs. Charles stands with us at the door. After a minute I can see her kinda slump against the frame.

"How you doing, Mrs. Charles?" I ask.

"I'm doing alright, Johnquell. I appreciate you asking. What are you two doing out of school?" She's keeping an eye over our shoulders to see when the cop's coming back.

"You oughta see the hot mess we got for a sub. I had to take a walk or I was gonna pop that dude in the mouth." I didn't mean to dump this on Mrs. Charles when she's sick but it just spills out. "Dude acts like he knows everything and today he even asked me why I don't speak English."

"What?" Mrs. Charles is standing up straight now. She puts a hand on my arm.

"He told me to read my paper to the class and then he's like, 'How come you can write in English but you talk like a gangster?'"

"He said that to you, in front of the class?"

"No, after class, when I was going out the door."

Mrs. Charles leans against the doorframe again. I shoulda kept my mouth shut, just come to see her, see how she's doing, and left it at that.

The cop comes up just then and says, "Well, these boys don't have any record on them, so I'll just let it go this time. No point in my dragging them back to school myself so close to the end of the school day and having to fill out the paperwork. Ma'am, could I get your full name, too, please?"

Mrs. Charles spells out her name and the cop puts that in his little book.

"Now, you boys do what you need to do here and head right on back to school. If I catch you out here walking in any other direction before the end of the school day, it'll be a $186 ticket for truancy. Got it?" He squints at us like he means business but with his scrawny neck and his thin brown hair blowing in the breeze he doesn't look like he could hold us to it.

"Bye, officer. You have a blessed day," Mrs. Charles says as she opens the screen door all the way to let us in.

Her house's neat and orderly, nothing out of place, except there's a few bed pillows and sheets on the couch. There are family pictures

on every wall, from old-time black-and-white ones, to some in color
that got a younger Mrs. Charles and what must be her husband and
three children. She sits down on top of the sheets and asks us to sit
down too. Taco picks the chair closer to the couch so I take one by the
window.

"Tell me more about this substitute teacher," she says, looking at me.

"It's nothing, Mrs. Charles. I shouldn'a even brought it up. Don't
worry about it," I say.

"I do worry about it. I mean, of course you know how I feel about
how important it is to use language that's appropriate for the particular
situation, but he really disrespected you."

"I'll make sure he gets the message," I say.

Taco laughs.

"How are you going to do that?" Mrs. Charles looks worried now.

"Don't worry about it," I say. "We just came here to see how you
are. Did you hear anything back yet?"

"Johnquell, Taquan," she says and I know it's gonna be something
bad because she's using our names. "The tests won't be back for a couple
more days but the doctor told me that he wants me to prepare for an
intensive treatment." She's holding onto her knees and squeezing them.
"He said I needed to be ready to go in as soon as the weekend."

"It cancer?" Taco ask. His voice is real tiny.

Mrs. Charles's mouth clenches down and she looks to the side, like
someone in the next room called her name. "We'll see," she says.

She's tired, I can tell, so when she starts talking again I know it's just
to set us up to leave. "Taquan, what will you be doing this summer?"

Taco he's squirmy by nature and her question sure enough makes
him shift around in his chair like he's seven, not seventeen. "I'ma get a
job, Mrs. Charles. Fill out my applications for next year." He doesn't
look her in the eye, though.

"Taquan, you know you're a smart boy, right? Don't you go wasting
everything you've learned. You've got to stretch yourself, reach higher."

She reaches out her hand toward the end of the couch, like she could touch him. Instead she just pats the cushion. "You do those applications right and soon, you hear?"

"Yes, Mrs. Charles." He looks down at his shoes but then he pricks up a bit and says, "Maybe you can help me some this summer? I can come by, help with the yard or whatever else you got needs doing. And then you can help me."

"That would be nice, dear. Let's do that." Sounds like a plan, so I stand up. Mrs. Charles stays on the couch. She looks up at me and says, "How about you, Johnquell? You're still headed to Madison, aren't you?"

"Yeah, I'll be there. Long as I don't get myself expelled for popping a sub." Mrs. Charles's eyes get all big, so I laugh and I wave my hand at her and say, "Naw, Mrs. Charles. You know I ain't doing that. I'm just messing with you."

She gives me that one-eye scowl she always does to show she's serious and she says, "Don't you waste this opportunity, Johnquell. You've got a bright future ahead of you. Don't you waste it on foolish pride or anger. There's a reason both of those are sins." She gives each of us a hard look and points at me then Taco. "Listen, I've seen it more than a few times. A smart young person gets so close to college and then does something to ruin their chances. Success can be scary. You have to be brave, both of you. You're the future."

We nod and Taco gets up to go too.

Mrs. Charles starts to stand up but she gets all shaky, so I grab her elbow. "Why don't you just stay there?" I ask but she keeps trying.

"No, I've got to see you boys out. Being a little tired is no excuse for being rude. Plus, I've got to lock the door behind you. You never know what kind of hoodlums might be wandering the neighborhood when they should be in school," she says, smiling at us. At the open door she puts her hands up on our shoulders, like the youth pastor used to do after Sunday school, blessing us students before we left for home.

"Hey, we're going to come by again soon. You let us know if you need anything," I say quick. "Right, Taquan?"

"Right," he says. "You think of something I can do around the yard," he adds, looking around at her lawn, which is already short. Besides the grass, there ain't but a few scraggly bushes along the bottom of the window. "Or inside. I can do inside too."

"Yes, you boys go on now," she says, giving us a little push with those tiny hands of hers. "I'll see you soon."

✺

"You may remember, class, that yesterday Mr. Braxton read his paper on the riot at the Long Binh Stockade in August of 1968. Today, I want to talk with you about my own experience. I hope you'll agree it's a rare opportunity to have a piece of living history in class."

A piece of something, that's for sure. Last night I couldn't fall asleep, thinking about what I was gonna say in class when he "corrected" my "misconceptions," so I woke up mad.

Mr. Discharge is one of those walking teachers, wandering around the room, his hairy white hand dragging and tapping on people's desks while he talks. I feel him coming up behind me and sure enough, he taps on my desk with two fingers when he gets to the "living history" bit. I look up at him and he looks right back at me, not blinking, like we got a staring contest going on.

"Long Binh Stockade was set up to accommodate soldiers and the occasional civilian who had committed crimes while overseas. Most of these were drug-related, going AWOL, or stealing, but there were others who were in there for more serious offenses, like attacking an officer. Before 1968, there were few such attacks. But 1968 was a kind of turning point, when military discipline began to fray, more and more soldiers started going AWOL, and the fragging really started."

"What is that?" asks Maddie. She's up at the head of the class, literally and grade-wise. I got to look at her and her big orange pony tail the whole time.

"'Fragging'? It comes from the weapon known as a fragmentation grenade. Can anybody guess what a fragmentation grenade does?"

"It breaks into fragments when it explodes?" says Kelly. She's all pushed up into her desk like she's hanging on Mr. Discharge's every word.

"That's right, Ms. Dixon. And those fragments, of course, rip thousands of little holes in the enemy's flesh. It's a very effective weapon. The word 'fragging,' however, came to mean a soldier killing another soldier from the same army. In Vietnam it especially meant a rank-and-file soldier killing an officer, and particularly—and statistics back this up, Mr. Braxton, so don't get 'up in my face' about this—a black soldier killing a white officer."

Dude's making those quote marks with his fingers when he's saying "up in my face." He's in between the farthest rows of desks on the left, right across from me, but I only look out of the corner of my eye. I'm folding an old bus transfer I found in my history book over and over to see how small it can get. "I ain't in your face," I say.

"What's that, Mr. Braxton?" he asks. He got this real eager sound in his voice, like he's hoping for a fight.

Now I do look at him. "I said I ain't 'up in your face.'" I make the finger quotes when I say it.

Mr. Discharge studies me a second and then says, "Good," and starts walking again. He musta done five laps around the room already. "So, anyway, fragging. It didn't necessarily mean the attack was carried out with a grenade. I knew one lieutenant colonel who walked into his hooch and got shredded by a nail bomb that had been wired to go off when the door opened. Others were shot at, sometimes in battle so the attack would be covered up. It was a form of revenge, for a supposed insult, or because the soldiers didn't trust their commanding officer to make good decisions on the battlefield. It's an overlooked fact about the war in Vietnam that fraggings or attempted fraggings happened thousands of times and that the killings were fueled by the rank-and-file soldiers' knowledge that the antiwar movement back home was getting stronger. Every protest back home meant another officer dead overseas, in my estimation."

Mr. Discharge is back at my desk again. He puts his hand on my shoulder and says, "Now, in Mr. Braxton's paper we heard a lot about the racial tensions around the Long Binh compound and he was right. Things were tense." I feel like he's trying to turn me to make me look up into his face, but I don't. The room shrinks in, like it's just him and me, and the puke green walls feel like they're starting to lean in on us. I shrug him off hard.

Mr. Discharge stands there for a second, then moves on and starts talking again. "Unfortunately, even in an army where there is no color, some people saw fit to bring color into it. Speaking from my own experience, it wasn't easy being considered suspect by the men just because of the color of my skin. I was called 'chuck' and 'dude' and 'cracker' all the time. Black soldiers were slow to respond to orders from a white officer or MP. And it wasn't just simple disrespect. As we know from the phenomenon of fragging, it could get deadly.

"And so, what about the dap? The dap wasn't just a sign of solidarity as we heard in Mr. Braxton's paper. There was this time, an altercation, we'll call it, in the mess hall. This was just before the jail riot, actually. There had been some tension there in previous weeks over the behavior of the cooks and servers in the cafeteria line. They'd be slinging the slop like normal and then suddenly some 'brother' would come up in the line and they all would set down their spoons to do the dap. Next thing you know, the line is backing up, down the corridor and out the front door, because they had to run through the whole five-minute routine, like they hadn't seen each other in years."

"Five minutes?" this kid named Dylan says, like he didn't hear the very same thing in my paper yesterday.

"Yes, five minutes. Now imagine what that would make you think. You'd think, 'I sure don't want to get caught behind a black man in line, or worse, two or three black men.' Just so we can get some perspective on that, Mr. Braxton, why don't you watch the clock and tell us when five minutes are up." He's looking at the watch on his wrist and got the pointer finger of the other hand raised. "Starting . . . now."

I don't say anything, just look up at the clock. Like I wasn't already counting the minutes 'til I could get out of here.

"Now, in the army, it's just like you in the cafeteria: you've got about twenty minutes to get and eat your lunch, right? If you don't get your tray, find a seat, and chow down, you're out of luck, with nothing else until dinner. Imagine if every time two cheerleaders saw each other in the lunch line they did some kind of pom-pom routine that took five minutes and kept you from getting your food."

Maddie and some other girl from the cheerleaders give each other a high five and laugh, like they're going to try that or something.

"Right, ladies?" He gestures with one of his big hands like he's handing Maddie and the other girl something. "So there was some tension in the mess hall. The week before, there had been some shouting and pushing that almost broke into a real fight, so a few of us MPs had been posted there to make sure the situation didn't escalate. We were under orders to detain anybody who kept the line from moving along. Our CO left it up to our discretion what that meant." He's up leaning on the desk again, finally staying still, looking up at the fluorescent lights.

"So, one soldier gets halfway down the chow line and comes to this cook, a guy named Curtis who happens to be the main source of the Black Power propaganda circulating on base, and the soldier starts laying some dap on Curtis. I'm across the room, by the door, so I can see Curtis's face behind the counter. He looks right at me the moment he and this soldier—I think his name was Frederick—start up and I know he's doing it to tick me off, right? So I move in and tell them to stop. But they don't stop, they just slow down a bit and Curtis just keeps looking at me. So I tell Curtis he's under arrest and call over another MP to go behind the counter and take him away. Before the other MP can get there, though, Frederick takes a swing at my head and all hell breaks loose. All of a sudden, soldiers are fighting and knocking food everywhere. Benches are flying. I radioed in some backup and we arrested over a dozen of the worst offenders. It took three days before anybody could eat in the mess hall, the place was so broken up. After that orders came down from the brass that the dap and all other signs of black culture had been banned."

"Did you get hurt?" asks Kelly.

Mr. Discharge comes back to earth and smiles at her. "No, I was fine."

"What happened to Frederick and Curtis?" asks Dylan.

"Well, they were arrested, among others. I know Curtis was in the stockade when the riot happened, because ultimately he was one of the prisoners charged with inciting it. He was court martialed and served some time. Frederick, I don't know specifically, but I'd guess most of those arrested probably served some time, the ones that deserved it."

"Time's up," I say.

"Excuse me?" Mr. Discharge says. He checks his watch. "That wasn't five minutes."

"I know. But time's up because I want to know, how many of the soldiers got arrested was black?"

"See, this is what I'm talking about," dude says, opening his arms wide to the class and then letting them fall to his sides. "Why does everything have to be about race with you people? Why does it matter how many of them were black or white or green or whatever?"

"It matter a lot. It matter 'cause they probably had families back home waiting on them."

"And how is that different from a white soldier serving time and missing his family?"

"We get more time, dude. We get it worse." See, this is why this fool can't be teaching U.S. history. He don't know the first thing about it.

Mr. Discharge folds his arms across his chest. "Don't you tell me," he takes a second to look at the attendance book on the desk before he continues, "Johnquell, that they didn't deserve it. Discrimination isn't some kind of pass, some kind of 'Get out of jail free' card. You do the crime, you serve the time, end of story. It doesn't matter if you feel like your CO doesn't appreciate you because of the color of your skin or if you feel like your little toes are getting stepped on because you can't wave your Black Power flag around the barracks or because you don't get Nipsey Russell on the USO tour. It just doesn't matter. You still did the crime."

He's looking right at me so I say, "I ain't done nothing, Lieutenant Cracker."

The room goes cold. I hear Maddie squeak out, "What?" and Alex say, "Hey, you can't call him that!"

"Just did," I say to Alex. I get up out of my desk, pick up my book bag, and step out the door.

I hear the sub getting on the phone to the office, but I don't care. I make my way to the front door and walk out. They're going to come try and stop me, maybe, but so close to graduation, I ain't going to sweat it.

Prelude to a Revolution

Loretta could always tell when John was steamed. He didn't yell or even grumble like other men she knew. He fixed things. On this Saturday afternoon, he was checking all the cabinet door pulls in the kitchen. One had lost a screw this past week—it had worked itself loose and rolled away into a dark crevice under the sink—and now he was checking every other one for good measure.

"What you mad about, John?" Loretta asked him. She was peeling potatoes at the sink. She didn't even need to look at him to know he was at the broom closet now, tightening the door handle.

"I don't know what you mean." He kept on, every cabinet door closed with a wallop. Bang. Fixed.

"I mean, I'm trying to put some dinner on the table and you decide this might just be a fine time to fix the kitchen cupboards. What's going on with you? Don't you have some work to do for the Party right now? Maybe standing on the street corner with a tin can, begging spare change off all those white boys who work downtown, so you can feed some more children that ain't yours?"

John slapped the last cabinet shut, his hand dark against the glossy white paint of the door like punctuation on a page. He turned and waved the screwdriver at Loretta and gave her a shake of his head.

"Don't you start that again," he said. He sounded more tired than angry. "Those are our children. They're our community's children and they need our help. If you could trouble yourself to come to Wednesday night political education class, you might have a bit more revolutionary consciousness."

She turned to look at him. "Wednesday nights is church. And it's Jesus's revolution I'm concerned about. Won't be no Huey P. Newton checking your soul at the Pearly Gates." Loretta turned back to the potatoes. She admired John's idealism back when they were dating, how he wanted to be somebody, make changes. Then she married him and the children came, and it seemed to her his idealism turned the corner at a street called Foolishness. Shouldn't a man with a wife and children be home in the evenings to protect his family? To discipline the children? Especially in these times.

John put the screwdriver in the drawer next to the sink. The wood squealed when he shut it. Long ago, the sink's cabinet frame had started to sag and now the drawer listed a little to the left.

"Hmm. Needs some that wax, huh?" She smiled up at John and touched his face with her hand still damp from peeling. "You got something on your mind that I'll bet doesn't have one whit to do with my poor, unsaved, revolutionary soul. Come on, tell me."

He pulled her to him, her back to his belly, so they both faced the sink. She felt him take a deep breath. Although she had finished rinsing the potatoes a full minute before, a plump drop of water was curling at the head of the faucet, ready to fall.

"Maxwell and I got into it this afternoon at HQ," John said.

"'Bout what?"

"'Bout his woman problem."

Loretta turned then to look John in the eyes. "Now didn't I tell you? Sure as I'm breathing, I knew James was stepping out on Georgine."

John chuckled and shook his head again. "No, not that kind of woman problem. If half the evil you thought was going on in the neighborhood was really going on, your sweet Jesus would have done brought his holy kingdom down on Third Street already and crushed us all."

"What kind of woman problem does Maxwell got then?"

"I think it's more like my woman problem."

"John Ulysses S. Grant Tibbetts! You better be telling me a story." Loretta pulled out of his arms altogether and went to get the buttermilk from the refrigerator.

"I wonder sometimes where you get your ideas about the sexes, Loretta. You think the only truck a man and a woman can have with each other is a carnal sort." He reached for her arm and pulled her back to him. "I'm talking about what's going on in the Party. I raised the issue at the weekly meeting yesterday that somehow our supposedly revolutionary organization has got all the sisters down in the kitchen and all the brothers at the front of the house making all the decisions."

"Well, if the brothers could be trusted with the cooking, maybe something could change. I'd guess some of them can't tell a frying pan from the back of their hand. And I know you wouldn't put up with them serving lumpy pancakes to the children of your beloved lumpenpotatertot."

"Lumpenproletariat."

"Lumpenproletariat. I know that. It's not like I don't hear you talking about it night and day. I just got potatoes on my mind. Now get out of my way so I can finish up here." She flicked a dish towel at him. "Go find your children—and I mean your children, the ones you and me made—and tell them to come in and get washed up for dinner."

A while later the children did come in—Alston, Leo, Bee-Bee, and Gloria. Loretta loved the sounds of their feet clomping through the house, their sudden laughter.

Six-year-old Alston was helping Gloria into her high chair. Alston looked like a miniature version of John, both of them with a long nose framed by high cheekbones and eyes that shone—with intelligence or sometimes mischief.

"That mud on your face better not be from under Miss Ava's bushes," Loretta said. "You know she won't stand for you crawling around under there messing up her yard. Come here."

"Is it buttermilk gravy, Mama?" he asked as Loretta wiped at his nose.

"It is."

"Good," Al said.

"Guh," Gloria cooed back.

Al smiled. "Gloria likes buttermilk gravy too. Dontcha?" He went to tickle her and she squirmed away from him, giving him one of her squeaky baby laughs.

"Guh!" Gloria said. She was just one the month before last but she was already trying to talk like her big brothers.

At the end of supper—greens, chicken fried steak, mashed potatoes, and gravy—Loretta said, "I don't know why any woman would complain about feeding children. This is the best part of my day, sitting here just a minute before I have to get up and start on the dishes, looking at the faces of you and the children and knowing I fed you all real good, fed you food I made with my own hands. I don't know why any woman would complain."

John let his knife fall with a clatter onto the edge of the plate. It slid to the table and a gob of tan gravy shot across onto Leo's shirt. Leo made a wide *O* with his mouth and Al and Bee-Bee laughed.

"Cut it out, Leo," John said.

Loretta half stood, about to deal with the mess but instead sent Al. "Alston, you go help your brother clean that up. Use a touch of that yellow soap, too."

The two boys went off to the washroom. Bee-Bee started dancing her fork along the rim of the high chair's wooden tray and humming some made-up tune. Loretta could hear the metal pail knocking on the washroom's tiled floor.

John was running his fingers back and forth along the edge of the table, a sturdy pine one they had inherited from John's mother when they first married.

Loretta looked at John and said, "What?"

"What, what?" he said.

"Don't act like I can't read you, John Tibbetts. We been together too long for that."

He sighed. "Fine. Why is it you take what I said about all the women in the Party being left to do the cooking like some kind of personal judgment on you? Nobody's saying that it's counterrevolutionary for you to enjoy feeding your family. I'm not even saying that I want to do the cooking here at home."

Loretta tilted back her head and laughed. "Good Lord, preserve us. I think once a year on Mother's Day turns out to be plenty."

"I just don't know how we can wave our flags and chant our slogans and say that the Black Panther Party stands for the liberation of all the people if only half the people's getting to make decisions. Does the cooking need to be done? Yes, of course. There couldn't be any children's breakfast program without somebody down there in the kitchen." His voice rose and Bee-Bee stopped her song and looked up. "The cooking is important work, worthwhile work, work with dignity. And, yes, a woman should be proud to do it."

Loretta started shaking her head. The man was on his soapbox good and high now. John reached out and put a hand on her shoulder. "But the fact is," he said, looking Loretta in the eye, "a man should be proud to do it too. All I'm saying is, if we want real justice in this society, we got to start with our own selves. It's 1972 and we should know better by now."

Loretta said, "You been hanging around with them white university students too much. You beginning to sound just like them."

He let his hand drop from her shoulder. "It's not just white university students, Loretta. Brother Newton's saying the same thing, that black men can't be using what little privilege we got in order to turn around and oppress black women."

"Well, I'm glad Brother Newton got your back, because let me tell you something. Maybe you ain't noticed yet, but your little white friends in the Students for a Democratic Society are at the top of the food chain. They don't got a worry in the world. The revolution goes great, then fine and dandy, they're going to come out on top of this new world you all are trying to create. Revolution fails, then that's just fine too, because they're still going to be top of the heap. And one of their daddies still going to be your boss at A. O. Smith."

John's mouth clenched and he took in a harsh breath. "You think so, huh? Well, then, it's too bad you didn't marry James Maxwell when you had the chance. You two got more in common than you realize." He pushed his plate away from him, stood up, and went out the front door.

Al and Leo stood in the doorway of the bathroom, silent and open mouthed, and watched their father go. A curl of cool late-May air snaked its way across the living room, into the kitchen, and around Loretta's ankles, prompting her to get up to get her sweater from the pegboard near the door. She pushed open the screen with her shoulder and its rusty metal spring strained back at her weight. The lilacs in Miss Ava's yard were blooming and the smell drifted over to Loretta, sweet and green. She watched John walking down Third Street, going in the direction of the Party offices, his tall form hunched over and dark against the emerging twilight.

Gloria began to cry and Bee-Bee called, "Mama, the baby wants out now." Loretta stood at the door another minute. She watched a car go by in the street, the driver's face shining for a split second in the orange glow of the car's cigarette lighter. Then Bee-Bee called again, "Mama!" pulling Loretta back to the work at hand.

❁

It was nearly eight o'clock and dark when John got to HQ. The Party office's windows were reinforced with wire mesh, so from the outside the yellow light of the front room seemed broken into a thousand smaller lights, like a church window. John took the steps two at a time, feeling the change in his pocket thumping against his thigh as he did. Once inside, he took that change—two quarters and a nickel—and

gave it to Betty Simmonds, who was working reception. She smiled at
John and dropped his coins into a can in the top drawer of the beat-up
metal check-in desk, then locked the drawer with a key.

"Thank you, brother," she said. At age fifty or so, Betty was the
oldest woman in the local branch. She sat at this desk just about every
evening, watching over the rest of them like a plump mother hen. Her
sharp eyes never seemed to miss a move.

"The chairman in here?" John asked her. Franklin MacRay was the
chairman of the branch and John was his deputy.

"Yes, he's in his office. Working on the weekly report to national, I
expect." She waved him toward the open door behind her. HQ was a
former duplex, converted into meeting rooms and offices. Franklin's
office had been a bedroom when the Party took over the place. The
pink flowered wallpaper was now covered in many places with posters
and news clippings.

John knocked on the doorframe. "Frankie, you got a minute?"
Franklin was typing at a desk piled high with manila folders, newspapers,
and envelopes. Two overflowing ashtrays were lined up along the left
edge and the black typewriter occupied the only other surface not
stacked with paper. Franklin put his cigarette in his mouth and stood to
lay some dap on John. They had their own routine, with three slaps of
their hands. "One for you, one for me, one for us," they said.

"Good to see you, brother. You're just in time to help me, uh, report
what went down at the weekly meeting between you and Maxwell. I
been sitting here trying to think how to put it." Franklin pulled another
chair from the corner over to the desk. "You're going to be glad to help
me out with that, I'm sure." Franklin's ample face wore a look of amused
forbearance. The rivalry between James Maxwell and John was a constant
refrain in Party business, one that had its roots back in high school,
when Loretta dated Maxwell for a while.

John gave him a smile. He wove his long fingers together like a
preacher or a professor about to intone on a matter of importance.

"Put down that Brother Maxwell continues to hold onto patriarchal, bourgeois attitudes about the roles of the sexes. And that you're assigning him to the kitchen for reeducation purposes. Indefinitely."

"Ol' Maxwell sure gave you a hard time, didn't he?" Franklin reached over and dumped one of the ashtrays into the wastebasket next to the desk, sending up a cloud of ashes that stuck to the knee of John's pant leg. "Sorry about that," he said, watching John brush the ashes away. "But you got to admit, it's a tough nut to crack, the role of women." Franklin massaged the top of his bald head with his fingertips, as if he might be trying to work a solution out that way. "On the one hand, like you say, we got to start bringing the sisters into leadership or we can't rightly say we're a revolutionary organization. On the other hand, that's not something the sisters are all that comfortable with. Sister Luella Hughes said to me the other day she couldn't imagine ever trying to tell her husband what to do, not here nor at home."

"Well," John said, "she didn't seem to have any trouble telling him her mind when he declared he was going to give 30 percent of his salary to the Party." They laughed at the memory of that meeting last September. Back from a trip to Madison to convince the university students to part with some of their financial aid money for the liberation of the masses, the leadership was feeling a little high off their success—over $2,000 collected—and several Party members had made some rather generous pledges of their own.

"That's true," Franklin said. "Luella smacked him so hard it was like she was trying to take 30 percent off of him." He shook his head and let off a whistle that sounded like a bomb falling. He turned back to the typewriter and positioned his hands over the keys. "Now, what am I supposed to say in this report?"

"Tell them we are in the process of self-examination on the matter of equality of the sexes in leadership. Tell them we're going to make some changes."

"Changes like what?" Franklin wasn't typing.

"I think you should ask Marla Lampkins to lead the next meeting."

"What does she know about leading a meeting?" Franklin asked.

"She's a good organizer and she's tough." John leaned in to make sure Franklin was paying attention. "Listen, any woman who can get that bastard store manager over at Mitchell Foods to give us all the orange juice the kids in the program can drink for a whole year can surely run a two-hour meeting of ten men."

"That's ten men think they know everything and aren't used to being told any different by someone wearing a skirt," Franklin said, cocking an eyebrow.

"I'll tell her to wear a pair of pants, then," John said, then leaned back to watch Franklin think it through. John could hear the city bus pass the building heading north, making the office window rattle as it passed. "So, we're good?"

Franklin pursed his lips and nodded. "Yeah, we're good."

☀

The next night, Loretta was folding laundry in the narrow living room, stacking clean towels and sheets on the coffee table. Bee-Bee and Gloria were in bed, but Al and Leo were still awake, making up emergencies for the imaginary firemen in their toy fire truck to attend to.

"Oh, no! Come quick! There's a big fire at Garfield Elementary School!" Al was saying. "All the books are on fire! Oh, no! And Mrs. Scott!"

"Alston," Loretta said. "Don't you talk about your teacher that way." Al was not a fan of his first-grade teacher, an older white woman Loretta was convinced didn't think black boys could learn.

"Yes, Mama," Al said. Leo was driving the truck along the thick braided rug in the opposite direction; Garfield and Mrs. Scott would have to take care of themselves.

Loretta could hear John on the phone in the kitchen. Who could he be talking to so late? She strained to hear what he was saying. The tone of his voice was silky—his first-date voice, his going to the store owner to see about food for the children voice. She knew that voice.

"Wee-oo, wee-oo, wee-oo, weeeeeeeee-oooooooooooooooooo," Leo called out, lost in his own emergency rescue.

"Leo, enough. You going to wake up your sisters," Loretta said. "You boys put that truck up and go to bed now." They made some small noises of protest but stood up anyway. She heard John laughing in the other room and called the boys back. "Hold up," she said. "Leo, Al, let's go say good night to your father."

She gathered the fire truck from Leo's hands and put it in the metal milk crate that served as the boys' toy box. Then she put an arm around each of her boys and walked them into the brightly lit kitchen.

"You got that right." John was smiling into the phone, light beaming off his cheeks and forehead. He was seated on the top step of the step-ladder in the corner, left there from his cupboard-repair endeavors the day before. With one hand he held the phone and with the other he held a candle, unlit and worn down on one side where he must have been rubbing it against the inner workings of the junk drawer to get it to stop squeaking.

"That's right, on Friday. Six o'clock," he was saying. "Yes, but wear pants."

—

"Course I'm serious. Franklin and I both thought that would help the brothers deal with you straight at the meeting."

—

"Course I take you serious. We all do."

—

"OK, well, that's Maxwell's problem then. Don't you put that on the rest of us. You know I know you're a force to be reckoned with, no matter what you're wearing."

—

"Mmm-hmm." His mouth was so close to the receiver, his lips grazed the green plastic as he spoke.

—

"A force of nature. A hurricane."

Loretta cleared her throat and said, "John."

John jumped just a little, like somebody poked him in a sensitive spot, and looked up.

"Sister, listen. I got to split. You let me know what else you need to get ready for the meeting."

—

"Mmm-hmm. You too. Peace."

He hung up the phone. "Hey, you guys going to bed?" he said, reaching out his hands to Leo and Al for a fistbump. "That's it." He took a minute to help Leo get his little five-year-old knuckles lined up just right. "That's how we do it. Yeah. Now give me a kiss and get out of here."

The boys did as he asked and said, "Good night, Daddy." Then he gave each of their behinds a swat, like he was starting off horses in a race, and they went toward the room they shared at the front of the house.

"Who was that?" Loretta asked, crossing her arms on her chest.

"Marla Lampkins." John stood up from the stepstool and tested out the drawer, pulling it in and out a couple of times. It didn't squeak anymore. He threw the candle into the drawer and closed it. "She's going to chair the next weekly meeting."

"And she called you for, what, fashion advice?"

"I called her. Franklin asked me to, to help her get ready. She's never chaired a meeting before, but I think she's going to pick up on it quick. She's a real fast learner."

"A force of nature, I hear," Loretta said.

They looked at each other for a few seconds, the overhead light now revealing the tiredness in John's face.

John kissed the top of Loretta's head and walked past her. "I'm going to bed."

Loretta stayed there in the kitchen for a good hour after John left, sitting on the stepstool and thinking things out.

When John woke the next morning at six he was surprised to find his mother-in-law in his kitchen. She was pouring herself a cup of coffee from the percolator on the stove.

"Alberta, what are you doing here?" he asked.

"Well, ain't that a fine way to greet your wife's mama," Alberta said, picking a piece of coffee grounds out of her cup.

"Sorry, Mother." He went over to her and kissed her cheek. "Where's Loretta?"

Alberta sighed. "She went down to the Party headquarters. She volunteered to help cook breakfast for those children and so here I am to cook breakfast for you and your children and see that you get off to work on time. Guess that make me a Party volunteer too. Or a draftee, more like." She smirked. Loretta sometimes made that same face, a lopsided pout.

"I'll be damned," John said.

"You sure will if you be cussing like that," Alberta said. "How you want your eggs?"

John couldn't think of any of the ways eggs come. "Any way is fine, Mother," he said, and went to get dressed.

On the bus up to the Smith plant he kept the day's newspaper folded in his hands. Party rules required that every member of the branch leadership read at least two hours a day, to keep up with the political scene. But John's thoughts were caught up in the current events at his own house.

"Borrow your paper?" the man in the next seat asked.

"All yours," John said, handing it to him. There was a cover story about a protest against the widening of Locust and Walnut Streets that he had been meaning to get to. The neighborhoods were organizing against the city's plans to bulldoze the houses and stores along those major east-west thoroughfares, and the Party was talking about getting involved. It might be a good opportunity to build a black-white alliance.

But he couldn't keep his mind on neighborhood politics for long. Instead, John swung between extremes, first wondering, with no small dose of skepticism, what had come over Loretta to make her suddenly so interested in the work of the Party. Then, pushing his skepticism aside, he allowed himself to fantasize about them working together to lead the branch, envisioning her taking over as administrator of the breakfast program, or maybe even deputy minister of information. She had a mouth on her, no doubt about that. With a little political education, something to radicalize her, she could use it for good.

⁂

Loretta was standing at the sink in the basement kitchen at HQ, her hand deep in a twenty-quart stock pot, scrubbing out the last of the grits, when Marla Lampkins came in from wiping down the breakfast tables. The heels of Marla's boots tick-ticked like typewriter keys as she made her way across the jelly-smeared tile. Take away the dirty towel thrown over her shoulder and she looked like something out of a fashion magazine, with her minidress and her high-heel boots and her sky-high hair.

"Getting down to the nitty-gritty, huh, Mrs. Tibbetts?" Marla said.

"I guess you could call it that," Loretta said, not looking up.

"Actually, I was riffing off something from Bobby Seale. He said, 'If you want peace and freedom, you got to get down to the nitty-gritty and don't miss no nits and grits.' I think about that a lot when I'm down here, how it's all the little things we do that build the revolution."

"I tell you, from what I seen and heard today, the Black Panther Party does more quoting of scripture and verse than a Baptist preacher in a month of Sundays." Loretta turned the pot over, pouring out the milky water into the sink. "I thought it was just my husband talked like that all the time, quoting Brother This and Sister That and Chairman Who-all."

Marla took the pot from her and began to dry it with the towel. "There's a lot of wisdom to be gained from memorizing the words of great leaders."

"I suppose. My husband sure thinks so, anyhow." Loretta turned to inspect the floor. "You all got a mop around here?"

"In the closet by the icebox over there." Marla pointed out a niche hung with a fading, green-striped curtain. She asked, "So, are you thinking of joining the Party now?"

Loretta hefted up the mop to keep the rag ends from dragging on the floor as she returned to the sink. "I'm thinking on it. My husband says there's a lot of things I could do to help." She turned the tap and let the water run until it was hot enough to steam, then filled the bucket.

Marla was looking Loretta up and down, with her head cocked to one side and her eyes narrowed. She straightened up and said, "There is a lot you could do to help. If you can commit to helping cook for the breakfast program three days a week, that would free me up to take on more sector organizing in the neighborhood."

Loretta set the bucket down on the floor and plunged the mop into it. "Actually, I was thinking about joining the Leadership Committee."

Marla made a sound like she was choking on a drink and then snorted, like whatever she thought she was holding back might still come shooting out her nose. "The Leadership Committee?" she said. "That takes time. You have to get to know the organization, our principles, what we stand for. The Party is a solid, established thing, with structures and rules and relationships. You can't just walk into a leadership position."

Loretta looked up from mopping long enough to make sure Marla was following her and said, "Seems to me people be walking into things—solid, established things they don't know nothing about—all the time."

Marla's lips parted and closed again. She looked toward the sink. The faucet had let loose a drop of water every few seconds since Loretta filled the bucket and now Marla went to it and turned it off with a yank. "Well, alright," she said. "You go ahead and nominate yourself then and we'll just see what happens."

"How do I do that? Nominate myself?"

"John knows," Marla said, turning to leave. "You should ask him."

※

After work, John walked back to the house from the bus stop so fast that he was out of breath and sweating when he arrived. All day at the factory, loading steel into the cutting machine, Loretta had been on his mind. She must have heard him coming up the wooden steps because she was there on the other side of the door when he opened it.

"Hungry?" she asked.

"About to starve slap to death," John said. "But lay a kiss on your old man first."

Loretta rolled her eyes at him but tilted her head back so he could kiss her. He did and then he pulled her close.

"What all got into you?" she asked, pushing him away. "That roach coach selling happy pills instead of sandwiches today?" She turned to go back to the kitchen.

He watched her walk across the room and the graceful swing of her hips told him she knew he was watching. "I'm just happy is all," he called after her.

The sound of his voice brought the kids out of the girls' bedroom where they had been playing. "I'm a monster!" Bee-Bee cried. "Daddy! Rah! I'm a monster and I'ma eat you!"

Bee-Bee charged at his legs with her hands out like claws. "Oh, no you're not," John said, picking her up. "Don't you know daddies are stronger than any monster?" He gave her a kiss and set her down. He patted Al and Leo on the heads and kissed baby Gloria, who was scooting after the bigger kids in her walker. "You all go back and play. I'm going to go see Mama."

In the kitchen Loretta was washing greens. "Dinner will be ready in about twenty minutes. Why don't you go wash up?"

"I think we have something to talk about first," he said. He was still smiling. "So, you went to volunteer at the breakfast program this morning. How was it?"

"Alright."

"Just alright?"

"I met your force of nature."

"Who do you mean?"

"You know who I mean." Loretta looked John square in the eye.

"You mean Marla?"

"Yeah, Sister Lampkins."

"So we're sistering and brothering now, are we?"

"Don't think too much on it." She waved a wet hand at him. "We been doing that in the church two thousand years before the Panthers ever got hold of it. Seems like your Party's just another kind of church anyhow, brother. You got your preachers, your commandments, your soup kitchens, your collection plates. You even got your eyes on a new kingdom where the poor people'll be running the place."

"So, you think we can get Jesus to become a Panther?"

"I don't know. Maybe he already signed up." She gave John a sly smile. "Chicago branch, most likely."

John laughed. Whenever the two of them got into an argument of some sort, one or the other would cool things down with a joke. Laughter saved them many times from going at each other tooth and nail, John was sure.

"So you're going back tomorrow?" he asked, coming over to wash his hands at the sink. "It's going to be a big day. We won't serve the children on Monday because of the holiday, so we try to feed them something special the Friday before."

"The breakfast program's alright, I guess." Loretta thumped the colander of greens on a towel on the counter, shaking the water off. "But I been thinking about what you said, about how all the women are in the kitchen while the men are making all the plans."

"And?"

"And I was thinking you been spending so much time on Party business it's like I never see you. Between work and meetings and organizing this that and whatever, you ain't hardly ever home anymore. And that ain't right." She dried her hand and reached out to him with it, keeping the other one folded across her waist. "I want to be with you, John. I don't want you getting all the meaning in your life from somewhere where I can't be."

Loretta began to cry then and John wrapped her up in his arms and let her. "Shh. Shh," he said, stroking her hair. "You can always come with me, baby."

"Yeah, but do you want me to?" She wiped some of the tears from her cheeks and looked up at him.

He pulled her in close and rested his head on top of hers. Course I do. Course I do."

"I want to nominate myself for a leadership position in the Party," she said, pushing against him enough to face him again.

"Leadership?"

Loretta extracted herself from his arms and wiped her eyes with a dish towel. "Yeah, I want to be one of those women you trying to line up to help make decisions."

John looked at Loretta, searching her pretty oval face for some clue about what had come over her, but it was set with what John had come to think of as her "done" look. As in, "I already done decided."

"I see," he said. "What position were you thinking of?"

"Well, I was thinking I could do something to raise money."

"Fundraising? You know that's not going to be easy. Businesses are afraid to give us money. The churches are afraid to work with us. We don't exactly got a lot of rich friends."

"I can do it."

"Well, I'm sure you can, but," he began but she was making that "done" face again so he stopped. "Deputy minister of finance is what you're aiming for then. That sound good?"

"Sound good to me." She smoothed her straightened bob where John's head had mussed it up.

"That position is vacant right now anyway, but I got to warn you, the minister of finance is James Maxwell."

"I guess we know why there ain't no deputy."

They both stood there thinking for a minute and then John clapped his hands together.

"Well, right on, sister. I'm going to go take a shower, and then we're going to eat, and then I'm going to write up your nomination."

❁

At the top of the stairs to HQ on Friday, John stopped Loretta. "Hold up," he said. "When we're in there, try not to talk too much."

"Why not? I thought that was the whole idea, letting the women talk."

"Maxwell's going to try to trip you up, you know? He'll say something to set you off and I just need you to keep it real cool. Don't let him get you all riled up. Cool as ice, OK, baby?"

Loretta was going to protest but something caught her eye and instead she pulled on the sleeve of John's coat to turn his attention toward the street. Two black-and-white squad cars were parked across First Street, in the service drive of the post office. John put his arm around Loretta and guided her inside.

"Somebody better call Old MacDonald," John said to Betty Simmonds, as they went in. "Some of his livestock's broke out the barn."

"Pigs?" Betty said, moving to the edge of the window to take a look. The wire mesh that covered all the windows in the place wasn't an undue precaution; it was to keep the glass from shattering on people inside during an attack. In the three years the Party had its offices there, HQ had been shot up, had its windows smashed, and books, food, and other supplies stolen in repeated raids by the police. And just a couple months before there was a failed arson attempt. Most of the Party suspected the FBI in that one.

John told Franklin about the cops and the two of them assigned some of the brothers to stations in and around the house. Just after Gene Everidge had taken his position up at the attic window, he called out, "All clear."

"They gone?" Franklin asked Gene.

"Yeah. The minute I got up there the both of them they just drove off."

"Let's keep a lookout at both the front and back doors," Franklin said, gesturing to Kwame Sutton and Mike Thomas to stay where they were. "And let's get this meeting started so we all can get out of here and enjoy the long weekend."

Franklin seemed to notice Loretta for the first time and gave her a fatherly smile. "Welcome, sister. John told me about the nomination." He patted her on the shoulder then pointed to the stairs. "Meeting's upstairs. I think everybody else is here."

The meeting room was the old master bedroom at the top of a tall, curved staircase. There was a big, oak dinner table in the center, surrounded by a mismatched group of chairs. Along the walls were stacked banker boxes with their contents labeled in black marker— Loretta could make out one that said, "Weekly reports, 1969-70," and another labeled, "Prison bus project"—and piles of posters and leaflets. Two pale blue Panther flags hung between the windows that looked out on the street.

Marla, James Maxwell, and seven other men were already seated around the table, talking, but they fell silent when John and Loretta came in. Once they found seats—Loretta at the end of the table nearest the door and John at the head next to Franklin—Marla stood to open the meeting.

Loretta did her best to keep up, but there were a lot of names and initials and organizations mixed in with the talk of finances and programs and upcoming actions. Marla seemed to have a handle on it all, though, and every time Franklin or John or some other man at the table started asking for comments or directing the conversation, she would firmly say, "I'm going to have to remind you, brother, that I'm the chairman of this meeting." In spite of herself, Loretta was impressed.

The last item on the agenda was the nomination of new Leadership Committee members. Marla introduced the item and asked for any nominations for vacant seats.

John stood. "I nominate Loretta Tibbetts to the position of deputy minister of finance," he began. "Although Sister Tibbetts is new to the Black Panther Party for Self-Defense, she has been an active supporter of our branch and a firm believer in its revolutionary work seeking the liberation of our community from economic and social oppression. Recently, she began volunteering in the children's breakfast program."

"Very recently. Like, this week," James Maxwell said to the man next to him, in a stage whisper loud enough to be heard at either end of the table.

Franklin said, "Brother Maxwell." And Brother Maxwell lifted his hands off the table as if to say, "What?" but he kept his mouth shut.

John continued, "She wishes to help the Party expand its fund-raising activities into new sectors and increase the number of women involved in the Party in general. She is a smart, loyal, brave, and capable sister and I hope you will join me in voting for her for this important position."

Loretta felt her cheeks flush. It was embarrassing to have John talk about her in front of all these people. His speech made her sound like some kind of hero. She looked across the table to where he sat. He winked at her.

Marla asked, "Can we get a second to the nomination?"

Loretta chanced a quick look around. Most of the men had their eyes on the papers before them. Lamont Elder leaned back in his chair, crossed his arms on top of his head, and stared at the ceiling.

"Can we get a second?" Marla asked again. "We need a second before we can move on to discuss the item." When there was no answer, she asked Franklin, "Is there any rule against the chairman of the meeting seconding a motion?"

Franklin shook his head. He looked like he was biting the inside of his cheek.

"Then I'll second the sister's nomination," Marla said.

Loretta didn't miss the look that passed between Marla and John then, or John's tiniest of nods and Marla's in return. She knew it for sure now. Something had gone on—maybe was still going on—between those two, something she wasn't part of, but she didn't have a second to puzzle it out because Brother Maxwell stood up to speak.

Sometimes when she looked at James, Loretta imagined what it would have been like if she had ended up with him instead of John. She thought about that now. The front of his afro was streaked with gray and he was getting a little belly on him, Loretta noticed. As if he could hear her thoughts, Brother Maxwell tugged on the corners of his denim jacket to straighten it before speaking.

"I want to remind the brothers of the committee that just last week Brother Tibbetts proposed an idea," he began. "That idea was that we bring some of the sisters into the leadership of the branch. And now look what we got here, two sisters, both apparently drug into this meeting by Brother Tibbetts himself. Some of you probably think we ought to congratulate the brother on his quick success. I, for one, won't be doing any congratulating. It looks to me like this is a clear conflict of interest on the brother's part.

"In fact, I feel it necessary to question Brother Tibbetts's motives. If he was honest with us, he would've just said, 'Under the guise of promoting equality of the sexes, of ridding ourselves of bourgeois attitudes, I plan to nominate both my wife and my mistress to the Leadership Committee, thereby making sure I earn my women's lib Girl Scout merit badge and still get all the tail I can handle.'"

Loretta closed her eyes. The room exploded in sound. She heard
Brother Elder laughing and John calling Maxwell out to prove it and
Franklin shouting, "That's enough," and Marla pounding on the table,
still trying to chair what was left of the meeting.

Help me, Jesus, Loretta began to pray. She felt a hand on her shoulder
and opened her eyes to see John. He crouched down to look her in the
eye, steadying himself with both hands on the arms of her chair. He had
an expression she hadn't seen on his face for a long time, maybe since
his mama died, a mix of grief and panic.

"Loretta, it's not true," he said. "You got to believe me. You know
the way Maxwell is."

Loretta stood up, pushing him off to the side. "I can't talk about this
right now," she said. She grabbed her coat from the rack and went down
the stairs and out the front door.

"Meeting over?" Brother Sutton called after her, but she just shook
her head, tears flying off her face as she walked faster and faster away
from HQ.

Loretta was half a block away when she heard the noise. First there
were two high-pitched whistles, each followed by a thud. In the twilight
she couldn't see what made the sound but she saw what came next: two
flashes of hot white flame that spread quickly across the porch of the
Party offices. She saw a figure open the door of the house and then retreat
inside, his arm on fire.

She began to run back, cutting across the lawn of the neighboring
house and toward the side yard of the Party offices. "Get out! Get out!"
she yelled, banging her fist on the lower windows as she went. "Get
out!"

When she turned the corner of the house she saw Brother Thomas
holding open the back door and shouting, "Come on! Come on!" to the
people inside.

Loretta ran up to the door and grabbed the wide collar of Brother
Thomas's leather jacket. "Where's John? The committee?"

"Sister, get away from the house," Brother Thomas said, pushing her down the short set of stairs.

She gripped the pipe railing and pulled herself upright. Through the open door she could see that the front of the house was all aflame. She could hear shouting, confused voices.

A couple minutes later a few Party members staggered out. First Brother Sutton, clutching his scorched arm and leaning on Sister Simmonds. Then, Brother Everidge, a stunned look on his face.

"The stairs," Loretta said, as two more people pushed past her.

Black smoke began pouring out the back door and the heat began to push those too close to the house like a heavy hand.

Loretta stumbled back to the alley behind the house, where Sister Simmonds was counting off heads and asking anyone who could answer to tell her who all was upstairs during the meeting. Neighbors were joining them from the surrounding houses and swelling their numbers. In the deep shadows of the alley, Loretta's eyes played tricks on her, imposing John's face on every man she saw.

Marla staggered into the alley, bringing with her a smell of singed hair and sweat. Loretta looked at Marla's shoeless feet, then up her blackened pants and shirt, to her face.

"I jumped over the railing. There wasn't time," Marla said to Sister Simmonds. "There wasn't time to do anything else. The whole room, it just went up." Marla covered her mouth with her hand.

Loretta's sight went dark for a minute, like someone had pulled a blanket over her eyes. She heard Sister Simmonds working her way through the crowd, saying, "Brother Tibbetts? Chairman MacRay? Has anybody seen Brother Tibbetts or Chairman MacRay?"

John couldn't be dead. They had plans, to have grandbabies and to sit on the porch in the two-seater swing and to laugh at each other's false teeth in cups by the bedside.

Loretta ran back toward the house. Through the doorway she could see the interior glowing, a raging orange against the city's murky half-dark. The heat struck her at the most animal level, telling her to get back, but she pushed against it this time, forcing herself to go in.

Inside, the wood of the house seemed to be speaking, hissing and snapping in an ancient language she almost understood. Disoriented by the smoke and heat, she felt how easy it would be just to lie down and listen to the wood talking. Then she came to her senses, dropping to her knees to get to the cooler air near the floor. She started crawling toward the base of the stairs but didn't get far before she bumped into someone moving in the other direction.

"Help me get him out of here," a man said. Loretta felt a hand fumble for her shoulder. It was John.

"Lor?" he said. "I got Franklin. Help me get him out of here."

Behind John, she could just make out another dark form on the floor. Loretta felt for Franklin's arm and together they pulled him toward the back door.

Brother Everidge saw them as they emerged on their knees, coughing, and called for others to come carry Franklin out to the yard. It was only when a couple of neighbor men came to help John and Loretta down the back steps that Loretta noticed that John was limping.

At Betty's direction, the neighbors sat John down in the back seat of Brother Darren Moten's Grand Prix. Loretta climbed in on the other side.

She leaned in to kiss his cheek and tasted soot. Up close, she could see that some of his hair had scorched off along the top of his head and into his sideburns.

"You OK, John?" she asked. She pointed to his leg.

John winced as he shifted it. "We had to jump. I think it might be broken."

Loretta reached for his hand and squeezed the long fingers. She held them for a minute, just feeling the relief of being alive.

Brother Moten opened the door and said, "Sister, if you can walk, I'm going to have to ask you to get out. Brother Franklin needs to get to the hospital."

Loretta looked out the window and saw three figures carrying Franklin toward the car. "Wouldn't he be better in an ambulance?" she asked.

Even in the smoky light of the alley she could see Brother Moten's expression of disbelief. He shook his head. "Sister, there ain't going to be no ambulance."

Loretta nodded. She got it now, how alone John had been in this work, how much they all were risking.

"OK," she said. She kissed John's hot face one more time and got out. "I'll find someone to give me a ride and I'll follow you."

Got the Ball

Misty got the ball and I wanted it. It was one of the only ones left with any bounce and I wanted to play foursquare. Most days Misty's nice but other times, like if she got a new dress or her mama did her hair different, she just does stuff to make everybody look at her.

"I got the ball! Nyah nyah," she called out to me. Soon as she had took it, she ran away across the little kids' playground, the one with the map of the fifty states on it that somebody sprayed "Obama!" on, not the middle-schoolers' one with the basketball hoops. I was standing on New York and she was over in Iowa or one of those states like a rectangle, far away so I couldn't catch her without running, but close enough that I could hear her just fine.

I got an 83 on the fifty-states test. I would of got 100 but I get the rectangle states all mixed up. Maybe she was in Nebraska.

"I got the ball and Nelly-Nelly doesn't! I got the ball and Nelly-Nelly doesn't!" She was out there singing that, over and over, shaking her booty, trying to do the dance we learned when I stayed over at her house that time and we watched Rihanna music videos real late until her mama made us turn the TV off.

Some other kids started watching us, to see what we would do. Duane yelled at me, "Nelly, she laughing at you," and he laughed too.

The wind was blowing the long fur on the hood of Misty's big ol' fancy winter coat and it was getting into her eyes. She had to hold the ball under one arm to get the fur out, so I ran right then, straight at her. I heard some of the other kids—Duane, Oceana, Kyra, and them—all go, "Ooooooooh," like they was about to see something.

Misty didn't run. She just stood there and I crashed into her. She fell on the ground and I snatched the ball right out of her hands.

"Now I got it," I told her. She just stayed down there looking up at me with her puffy white cheeks in her puffy white coat. "You better get up or your mama's going to whup you for getting your coat dirty." I didn't care about her stupid coat, I just liked the idea of somebody whupping her.

"I've never been whupped. My parents don't believe in hitting children." She sounded all grown when she said that.

"Well, you better get up anyhow," I told her but she stayed down there anyway. She was like that, staying on the ground just so the teachers would pay attention to her.

Mr. Salvador came over to see what was going on. He wasn't our teacher. He's some kind of teacher works with the special kids in the basement.

"What's happening here, girls?" he asked us. He's kinda fat and he was breathing heavy from jogging over. When he breathed out, he made big clouds of steam on us.

"Nothing," I said, 'cause nothing was happening right then, except Misty lying on the ground getting her fool self dirty and cold.

"Well, something's going on here and I don't want to see anymore of it. You got that?" he said, pointing at me then at Misty. He looked at his big watch and said, "Recess is over in eight minutes. If I catch either of you messing with the other one, I'll drag you both to the office. Got it?"

"Yeah," we both said. Misty was sitting up now anyhow.

✺

The next day on the playground was cloudy and cold. I didn't ask Misty to play with me 'cause I was still mad at her about the ball thing. I was hanging out with Oceana on the swings, not swinging for real, just twisting the chains and spinning back around. We were talking about Oceana's birthday party coming up and who is she going to invite. I was about to ask was she going to invite boys and girls or just girls, when all of a sudden I felt this heavy thing on my head and then this cold itchy stuff go down my back. I jumped up and looked and there was Misty, shaking sand off her mittens and laughing at me. I put my hand up to my head and felt the pile of sand she put there. I was so mad, I took a bunch of it and threw it at her. Then she got some more from under the swings and threw that at me and next thing I know all kinds of kids are throwing sand and I could hear Mr. Salvador's whistle and Miss Martin calling to the office on her walkie-talkie and I got piles of sand running down the back of my coat and I didn't care if I got in trouble or not.

✹

"Mrs. Peterburg?"

—

"Yeah, hello. This is Gloria Tibbetts, Johnelle's mother?"

—

"Yeah. How you doing?"

—

"That's great."

Mama was in the kitchen on the phone with Misty's mama. I was at the dining room table working on my math workbook. It was skip-counting by fours, like how many strings of beads you need to get to twenty-four if there's four beads on each string. There was picture of a string and a bunch of beads and I was thinking I could get up and go get my markers and color them in. I know that's not part of the homework, it was just for fun but I didn't want to miss Mama talking. She had told me she was going to call Misty's mama, tell her about my hair, how you can't do that to black hair.

"I know, I know. Kids. Suspended in the first grade. Back in my day they wouldn't of suspended nobody, just sent the both of them home to get the belt."

—

"Uh-huh. Well, I guess we're from different eras, then."

—

"Course I did. And a good thing too. I think it cleared her head a fair bit."

—

Out of the corner of my eye I saw Mama lean over to look at me but I kept my eyes on my workbook. I was coloring in the beads with my pencil. It wasn't as good as if I had my markers but I stayed in the lines. Mama was talking about my punishment, but what I wanted to know was was Misty going to get a whupping too. Otherwise, it wasn't going to be fair.

"No, not a belt."

—

"Mrs. Peterburg, I didn't call you to ask your opinions about spanking."

—

"Yeah, there is a lot of violence in the world but listen: Misty got sand in Johnelle's braids. We had just did them last weekend, so they were practically new. Now I got to take her in for another appointment and get them redone before the holidays."

—

"No, it's not that I want you to pay for it."

—

"About sixty bucks. But now listen, it's not . . ."

—

"It's not about the money."

That's not what Mama said yesterday when we got home. She's trying to act like she don't care now but yesterday she was pounding on the table saying, "And right before Christmas, too." And then she was pounding on my behind. She was madder than I ever seen her before. But I made her miss work to come get me from the school office and her boss don't like her to leave work early to deal with us kids.

—

"Sure, you could say it's partly about the time."

—

"Thank you. I'm glad you appreciate that my time is valuable. But that's not the main thing, it's . . ."

—

"Yes, I am a single mother. And a widow."

—

"Thank you. It's been a lot of years now, but, thank you. But what I'm trying to say is, it's a matter of respect, about the hair. You just don't mess with black women's hair."

—

"No, I don't think you do."

—

"It's not the same. You mess up your hair, it gets something tangled up in it or whatever, you just go comb it out."

—

"No, even gum. A black girl's braids get sand in them, it's a half-a-day project at least."

—

"Yeah, the time. But really, I just want you to understand that it's an issue. If Misty's going to go to a school that's mostly black kids, she's going to have to get wise about a few things."

—

"Mmm-hmm."

—

"Mmm-hmm."

—

"Nobody said anything about your 'commitment to the city' but you."

—

"Mrs. Peterburg."

I looked up then, to see was Mama mad but she was looking the other way. When Mama calls people by their polite name, it's for sure she's getting angry now. It was good she was trying to get Misty into trouble but now I started thinking if she made Mrs. Peterburg so angry I might never get to stay at Misty's house anymore. I got up and went to the kitchen but when I put my hand on her arm Mama just waved at me to go sit back down.

—

"OK, then, Judy."

—

"Judy."

—

"'The content of their character.' Right. I'm with you there, but . . ."

—

"We might not be all that different, but there is a difference. I think we both know that."

—

"Mmm-hmm."

—

"Mmm-hmm. Judy? I got to go now."

—

"OK. Yeah, you have a blessed weekend, now. OK. Bye."

Mama hung up the phone real hard and I heard her say, "Good Lord." I don't think Misty was going to get whupped after all.

🐢

"Stop your bouncing while I button you, Johnelle, or your collar'll be ruined." Mama was helping me put on my Christmas dress for the last day of school. The dress had a red skirt with black stripes, skinny ones and fat ones crossing over each other, and a shiny black top with long sleeves and a soft red collar. I was excited to be wearing my new dress but even better was Mama was coming to be a parent helper at the party. Most times she can't come see me at school, unless it's something after work or on the weekends, like that one time we did the tree planting around the parking lot, one tree for each grade.

We got to school early, before any of the other kids, 'cause Mama drove us. I'm in Room 213, with Miss Terrence. I showed Mama the red and green construction paper chains we hung around the classroom and the Christmas tree I made out of a Styrofoam cup and green gum drops, with one yellow one on top like a star.

"We can eat it after Christmas, if you want to. Not the cup. Just the candy part."

"That's real nice, Nelly," Mama said. It screeched when she slided it back on my desk.

Miss Terrence came over and shook Mama's hand and said, "Thanks for coming in to help, Mrs. Tibbetts. We don't get enough opportunities to see you."

Mama said, "I do what I can."

"It's a for-low day today," I told Miss Terrence. "So Mama can't go to work."

"A 'for-low' day? What's that?" Miss Terrence asked me.

"I think it's for-lowering the bills. Right, Mama?"

Mama bust out laughing. I didn't know what she was laughing about and so I said, "What? What?" until she stopped.

"'Furlough,'" Mama said while she wiped away a tear on her cheek. "She means 'furlough' day. More budget cuts at the county, you know. They're making all of us take ten days off this year without pay."

Miss Terrence let out a big sigh and said, "I know. It's a tough time."

"Nelly, that's the only time anybody said anything about furlough days that ever made me laugh," Mama said and she touched the top of my head. Her smile went all the way down to my belly. To Miss Terrence she said, "What can we do to help?"

Mama and me helped set up the tables with paper tablecloths and the sparkly candle holders we made in class out of pickle jars and glitter. Some of the jars still smelled bad but they looked pretty when we put the fake candles in them. I was the one who got to go around and turn on all the switches to make them light. When I got near the window I could see Mr. Michaels the janitor throwing some bags of trash in the big bins behind the school. No Christmas party for him.

Some of the other kids' mamas came in, too. Some of them were just dropping off juice and treats, but Gabby's mama and Misty's mama both stayed. Misty's mama had on a red skirt kind of like mine. "Plaid," Mama said the stripes were called.

"Well, look!" Misty's mama called out when she saw me. "We're twins!" She had on a long-sleeve black sweater, too, so we did kind of look like twins, I guess, except she's a white lady with light brown hair. She put her arm around me and turned us both so everybody could get a look.

Mama came over then from where she was putting out the plates and cups. She didn't look too happy to see Mrs. Peterburg. Mrs. Peterburg let me go when she saw Mama coming.

"Hi, Gloria."

"Hi, Judy."

"Johnelle's braids look nice."

"Yeah, they did a pretty good job on such short notice," Mama said.

I thought they looked way better than "pretty good." Miss Alice put in some special beads look like pearls for the holidays and Mama told Miss Alice she does the best braids in the whole city. So why she told Mrs. Peterburg they were just "pretty good" now I don't know.

"I talked with Misty about that, about the hair. She's really sorry."

Misty wasn't acting sorry. She didn't ever ask me to play or to sit by her at lunch. She always sat with Ella now and they watch me when I go by them in the cafeteria to put up my tray.

"I got her some books about it. I thought this was a real teachable moment, you know, and so we went to the library and got her that one called *Nappy Hair*, and then that one by bell hooks." Mrs. Peterburg put her hand on Mama's arm like she was about to tell a joke and she said, "Isn't it funny to think of her as a children's book author? I mean, I remember reading her in sociology class back in undergrad. Remember that one, *Ain't I a Woman*? I mean, really radical black feminist stuff, right? And now here's bell hooks of all people, writing books for little kids."

"I wouldn't know," Mama said to Mrs. Peterburg. Mama pulled her arm away and put it around my shoulders instead and said, "Johnelle, why don't you come over here and help me set those cookies out?"

Mama's voice sounded like she had one of those popcorn skins stuck in her throat, like it was itching her and she couldn't get it out. I guess she didn't like that bell hooks lady too much.

Mrs. Peterburg stayed where she was, looking salty but I don't know for what.

The bell rang and the rest of the class started coming in from outside. After everybody put up their coats and their book bags, Miss Terrence had us sit in the Morning Circle on the rug. Nobody but Miss Terrence was happy about that.

Lanie started everybody yelling, "We want the party! We want the party!" It was crazy. Tyrone even tried to take a cookie from the table and hide it in his hand but Miss Terrence caught him and made him give it to her. It took Mama and the other mamas to get everybody into the circle and hush up.

When we quieted down, we went around the circle and Miss Terrence told us to answer the question, "What are you looking forward to doing during winter break?" The talking stick this time was a penguin doll with a red Santa hat and a scarf on it. It's only your turn to talk when you're holding the talking stick. Even if it isn't a stick.

When it was Ella's turn she talked about how her family was going to Florida and going to the beach to get a tan. Next to her was Misty

and Misty said, "My family isn't going anywhere. I'll just be at home."
She kept twisting the white ball on the penguin's hat and then letting it
go, so it spun around while she talked.

Miss Terrence asked her, "Well, that's fine, but what are you looking
forward to?"

Misty didn't say anything. Her mama was sitting on a chair by the
other mamas, by the felt board. She said, "What about sledding, right?
Your dad is taking you sledding at St. Mary's Hill tomorrow."

Then Misty got a big smile on her face and said, "Oh, yeah. I'm
going sledding on my new sled. It's a toboggan and it can go really fast.
And presents."

A lot of kids said presents. I said presents and playing with my
cousins and doing movie night with my Aunt Bee-Bee where we're going
to wear our fuzzy pajamas and drink hot cocoa and marshmallows. I get
to stay over at her house unless stupid Jarrett is staying there because
Mama won't let me stay at Bee-Bee's if her no-account boyfriend is over
there.

After circle, we read our winter poems and showed the pictures we
made to go with them. And then Miss Terrence turned on the radio
station that plays all Christmas music and we finally got to have treats
and the punch Gabby's mama made with the white soda and juice.

Misty passed me on my way over to the cookie table. She gave me a
little wave, not up high, just a little one, and I felt my heart flip over one
time. I looked to see if her mama was watching or if my mama saw it,
but they were talking with the other parents, not paying the kids any
mind. I waved back and she smiled, just a little bit.

I went and sat with Oceana and Marcus and them, and we all had
snowman cookies and so Oceana told us we should play "Make a Rule."
It's a game she made up where you have to think up a rule for doing
something and this time it was "eat the snowman cookie all around the
outside first, going around and around the edges 'til it's gone." It was
hard to do because the cookie might break when you get too close to the

middle and then you're out. That happened to Marcus and he was
feeling so salty, he got up and said, "You all can keep your dumb baby
game," and he left. Marcus got to put himself in the coat room when he
gets angry. It's his cool-down room, Miss Terrence says.

I was getting close to the middle and I was being real careful so I
didn't notice right away when Misty sat down in Marcus's chair. Oceana
and Luis and Gabby all stopped eating theirs though, so then I looked
around to see why they stopped.

"Hi, Nelly-Nelly," Misty said, like she wasn't mad anymore. "Can I
play?" She held up her snowman cookie. It didn't have any bites out of
it yet.

I looked at Oceana and she shrugged. So I shrugged too and said,
"Whatever," like the high school girls in this TV show my sister Neitha
likes to watch. The girls are always making trouble for each other like
stealing each other's boyfriends and when they want to act like they
don't care they just shrug like that and say, "Whatever."

"You want to go sledding with me and my dad tomorrow?" Misty
asked me. She wasn't looking at me 'cause she was eating around the
snowman's hat. That was the hardest part, because it was the smallest.
She was doing it real slow and careful so it wouldn't break.

"Yeah," I said, 'cause I did. There wasn't anyplace to go sledding in
our neighborhood, so I never been. "I have to ask my mama though."

"Have to ask your mama about what?" Mama said. She had just
come up holding her coat and her hat.

I looked down at the table and started on my cookie again because
Luis was getting way ahead. "I wanna go swedding wif Missy." I was
thinking Mama might be mad if I said so, so I said it fast, without even
swallowing all those bites.

"What? Take that cookie out of your mouth," Mama said, tapping
on my hand. She didn't do it hard but hard enough to break the snowman's hat right off. It fell onto the table and the green sugar sprinkles
went everywhere.

"Mama! Look what you did," I said. "I lost now." I pounded the hat piece into the table until it was all crumbs. Luis waved his little bit of cookie at me 'cause he had got down to the very middle.

"Luis won," said Oceana.

Luis smiled at me. He was already missing both his front teeth. Maybe that helps you win cookie-eating contests.

Mama was zipping up her shiny brown coat and she said, "Clean that up, baby," like all the crumbs were my fault. "I need to go. I got a little shopping to take care of."

"Wait, Mama." I pulled on her sleeve. "I want to go sledding with Misty tomorrow and her dad, is that OK?" I said it real fast again. I put the edge of my cookie back in my mouth, not biting on it, just feeling it get all mushy and cinnamony.

Mama's face was squished up with that bump between her eyebrows she gets sometimes. She shook her head all slow and said, "You are a real puzzlement, child."

I was thinking that probably meant "no" but then Mama laughed, just one time, a low laugh with lots of air in it. Her eyes were twinkly and she was still shaking her head, but she gave me a pat on the shoulder and said, "You go if you want. Best keep your hat on though."

Revision

Stu Reid knotted his gray tie, with a few crisp motions he learned first in the army then gradually refined over thirty years of daily suiting up for his job at Elcor. He had loosened up a little since he started subbing at the high school, generally going only so far as a polo shirt and khakis with a belt. He liked suits, though, and missed the way they made him feel pulled-together and in charge. Maybe he would go back to wearing one when school started back up in a couple of weeks.

Veronica came into the bedroom carrying two empty laundry baskets. "When will you be back?" she asked. "I'm going to water aerobics in a bit and then I was going to go over to Stein's to see if they have that thing for the hose. A sprayer thing. The one you got last year is clogged already."

"Funeral's at ten. There's a lunch afterward."

"You're not staying for that, are you?" she asked. She dropped the baskets to the floor near the louvered closet doors.

"Of course not," Stu said, combing his thick silver hair. For a sixty-seven-year-old, he looked pretty good, he thought. He had a bit of a paunch visible under his white dress shirt, but he was still strong, with most of his own teeth and that good head of hair. He had just a few deep wrinkles cleaving his cheeks and brow. Veronica had told him once that they made him look even more solid, like how veins in white marble show the thickness of the rock.

"I don't even understand why you're going to the funeral," Veronica said as she began sorting the dirty laundry from the hamper into the baskets, lights and darks. "You knew the kid for what, a couple of weeks? Who's even going to know you're there?"

"I'll know I'm there." He pulled on his charcoal suit jacket. "The faculty, the other students."

"I guess," Veronica said, shaking her head. "You and your funerals." She swiped a few strands of her highlighted bangs out of her eyes and sighed. "I guess it doesn't matter whose child it is, it's still always such a shame when children die. He was, what? Sixteen, seventeen?"

Stu stepped around the laundry to get the shoe care kit from the top shelf of the closet and said, "I don't know. Something like that. Seventeen probably." He watched his wife sorting clothes while he settled onto the bed to touch up his shoes. He was glad she had started back at water aerobics. The pink T-shirt she had on was a little tight around the middle.

"His poor mother," Veronica said, hoisting one of the baskets onto her hip. "I just can't imagine. If that had ever happened to one of our kids, I wouldn't be here right now. You would've had to put me away."

☙

The church where Johnquell Braxton's funeral was being held was deep in the inner city, at Nineteenth and North Avenue. Sixtieth Street divided Milwaukee from Wauwatosa, the suburb Stu had lived in for most of his life, and the border was well populated with small stores— aquarium supply, hardware, ice cream—frequented by people from both sides of that line. He knew from the news that tax money had been used to stretch the economic vitality down North Avenue, and Stu could see the results in the clean facades of buildings in the 4000 blocks, painted in respectable tones of maroon, blue, and beige. The sidewalks around these revitalized buildings, with their wig shops, sports shoe outlets, and nail salons, were deserted though, even on a summer Saturday morning.

"Your tax dollars at work," Stu said to himself as he slowed to take a look at the street sign. He was at Thirty-Fourth Street. At Twenty-Seventh the tenor of the neighborhood really changed. The streets beyond were gap toothed. The crusty outlines of mortar and tar on adjacent buildings showed where factories, banks, and restaurants long since demolished had once stood. At Twenty-Fifth, Stu stopped at the light and watched a plastic bag scud across an empty lot until it smacked against the wall of the only functional operation on either side of the block, the plasma donation center. A line stretched out the door of the center, a couple dozen people all waiting to trade their vital fluids for forty dollars and a glass of orange juice. All men, Stu noted, all black men in various stages of uprightness, many wearing heavy jackets in the summer sun.

"Sure beats working," Stu thought.

He reached to turn the radio on, to Clark "Psycho" Sykora's show. He never missed a chance to get Psycho's take on what the crazy liberals in government were up to during his Saturday morning "Round Up the Usual Suspects" segment.

"Let's see who's getting the handout this week," Stu said, not noticing that the red Escalade in front of him had suddenly braked.

The blow wasn't too serious. Enough to get Stu's heart racing, but not enough to deploy the airbag. A fender bender. The front of Stu's car, nosed now under the trailer hitch of the Escalade, seemed to have done all the bending.

"Great. Just great," Stu said as he scanned the area. They were at Twenty-Third Street. A couple of teenagers on bikes watched from the corner. The bikes were too small for them, so their knees came up almost to their chests and their bright boxers hung out the back of their dark pants. Stu couldn't help thinking of the mandrill at the zoo, with its rainbow-colored behind.

Already, the driver of the other car was descending to take a look. Stu reached into the glove box for his insurance card. The man approaching was tall, big shouldered, black, wearing a suit and tie. He looked like he could be a defensive end in the NFL. The guy waited for Stu to get out.

"Hey, man, looks like you got the worst of it," the guy said, shaking his head.

It was true; the Buick's fender was caught under the hitch. The hitch was long and high up, like it was meant to pull an RV or a sizable boat.

"This is just great," Stu said, flipping up his cuff to take a quick look at his watch and then pushing his sleeve down. The teenagers were still watching them. Cars were starting to slow to take a look at the accident. Stu could feel the heat from their exhaust on the backs of his legs. "Of all days. I'm on my way to a funeral."

The other driver stood looking at the fender and didn't speak. He had his hands on his hips but he didn't seem angry. He reached up to rub his cheeks in a tired way.

"Look," Stu said. "I hit you so I know what the cops are going say, that it was my fault. Do you think you have any damage?" He followed the driver to the hitch and they both got into a half squat to look. The guy didn't seem to find this as difficult as Stu did. He must have been twenty years younger. His hair was shaved short with just a sprinkling of gray.

"No," the driver said. "Looks OK to me. I tell you what: let's exchange our information and then I'll help you get your car free. I got a funeral to get to myself. We can deal with this later."

"At Nineteenth and North?"

"What's that?" the driver said.

"Is the funeral you're going to right over here at Nineteenth and North?" Stu asked, pointing east.

The driver squinted at him and said, "Yeah. Water of Life Baptist."

"That's where I'm headed, too."

The driver cleared his throat and nodded once. "My nephew," he said. The man's mouth kept moving as a city bus went by, the bus creating a rumbling wall of sound that kept Stu from hearing anything else the man was saying. He could see the resemblance between this man and Johnquell now, something about the arch of thick brows over those deep brown eyes.

"I'm very sorry," Stu said when the bus had passed. He fumbled for something else to say. "He was a bright kid."

"You knew him?"

"A little, yes. I was his teacher."

"Oh, good. Good." Johnquell's uncle gave a half smile then, but it wasn't directed at Stu. His eyes had gone unfocused, like he could see right through Stu to something behind him. Stu looked over the other man's head, to a flock of pigeons that had just landed on the edge of the roof of the white brick building across the street, and waited for the moment to pass. A car honked, startling the pigeons away again and rousing Johnquell's uncle back to the here and now. "We better get this moving," he said, shaking his head again. "It's a hell of a thing."

Stu exchanged insurance information with the man—Leonard Tibbetts, with an address in the new condos on the south side of Wauwatosa, the controversial ones, the ones the older residents didn't want built—and Stu made sure to take some pictures with his cell phone. Leonard threw his suit jacket onto the driver seat of the Escalade and then pushed down on the Buick's hood and told Stu to put his car in reverse. He made it look easy.

The radio was still on when Stu rolled down the window to thank Leonard. Psycho was saying, "If they'd just get done shooting each other already we could get some developers in there with some tax incentives and . . ." Stu smacked the button on the dash.

"Well, that's that," Leonard said, rubbing his hands together to get the dust of Stu's car off of them. "I'll see you at the church."

Stu waited until he was in the parking lot of Water of Life Baptist to examine the damage more closely. The plastic bumper had a crack that extended almost all the way through and one side of the grille was busted out. He would need a complete replacement, but at least the car was drivable.

The parking lot was full of teenagers from the high school. He recognized a couple of them from the Advanced U.S. History class Johnquell had been in, suburban kids in summer dresses and nice pants, looking out of place next to the run-down corner store and the pawn shop with the security bars on the window. One of them, a girl with long blonde hair, waved to him. He waved back. He couldn't remember her name. On the whole, the Whitefish Bay kids looked underdressed against the crowd of black women in dress suits and fancy hats and little boys in ties. The blonde girl's bare shoulders embarrassed him.

The church was made of yellow brick, with a squarish steeple and a row of stained glass windows protected by a layer of thick, discolored plastic. A steady stream of people—young, old, black, white—was making its way up the stone steps and through the immense, carved wooden door.

The dim narthex smelled of old Bibles and furniture polish and sweaty bodies. Stu was carried along with the mass of mourners into a stately sanctuary lit by brass chandeliers and faux candle sconces. Nearly every pew was filled. He looked across the gathered heads, trying to find an empty seat, and caught sight of Gary, one of the teachers in the social studies department, a couple rows up on Stu's left. The spaces on either side of Gary were taken and he gave Stu a defeated shrug. Stu turned to see if there was a balcony, but a squat woman in a black sweater and white gloves put a hand on his arm and gestured to a narrow space at the end of a pew on his right. She had a stern, implacable face and stood at the end of the row until he obeyed her silent command. Stu thanked her but she just nodded once and moved on to the next visitor.

Stu shifted his eyes to see who he was sitting next to. It was a black girl, high school aged. She was leaning back with her hands in the pockets of her jeans, one leg stretched out under the pew in front of them, her foot jiggling in its sneaker as if she were trying to shake something off her shoe. Stu felt the vibration of her movement through the wood of the bench.

Leaning out into the aisle, Stu could see the silver casket at the head of the church. The lid was open and arranged along the hinge line was a row of framed photos or certificates—Stu couldn't tell for sure at that distance. He could make out the rough outlines of the boy's large face. Stu was a little surprised it was an open casket. The boy had fallen down the stairs and, by the principal's account, had gotten smashed up quite a bit. The undertaker must have done a good job.

It was just over two months ago the two of them had had their run-in in his history classroom. Stu had been called in as a long-term sub for a teacher who had fallen sick. Cancer was the rumor going around the teacher lounge but whatever it was, Stu had been engaged for the remainder of the school year. Johnquell was from Milwaukee and he was at Whitefish Bay High School as part of the voluntary integration program, but it didn't seem like he was trying too hard to fit in. Johnquell had written this paper about the Vietnam War that was full of distortions, trying to make the 1968 Long Binh Stockade riots into some kind of race war. When Stu told him he had been there, served as an MP in the very place and time he was writing about, the kid went ballistic. Like he knew better than Stu did what happened over there. Some kids were like that, thinking they could get everything they needed to know about a subject from a book or the Internet. You just couldn't argue with them.

An organist settled in on the stage behind the casket and the minister took his place at the microphone. "My friends, brothers and sisters in Christ," the minister began.

It had been a long time since Stu had been in church. He didn't know whether he believed any of this anymore. His parents had raised him as a Lutheran, but in high school he started questioning the whole thing, God especially. In his senior year, his science teacher called him a nihilist and jokingly told him he should read Nietzsche, which Stu did. Then he moved on to other writers, like Ayn Rand. He loved *Anthem*. By his first year of college, he was calling himself an atheist while on campus. Back at home for Thanksgiving, he kept his head down for grace but didn't say "amen." He hadn't known how to talk to his parents about not believing anymore, and anyway, not believing didn't mean he didn't want to be a moral person, a responsible person. He tried to live his life correctly, but this hocus-pocus, eternal life stuff just seemed like so much wishful thinking.

"Our God is an awesome God," the minister said. A middle-aged woman behind Stu shouted out, "Say that!" making Stu jump an inch off the pew. Stu turned to look at the woman but her eyes were pressed shut, as if she were resting after her outburst.

A woman in an electric blue suit was taking the microphone and the congregation stood. Stu stood too. With a robed choir for backup, the woman worked her way through a version of "There Is a Balm in Gilead" that Stu had never heard. He tried to follow along with the music in the hymnal but what the woman was singing didn't look anything like the notes on the page. He was surprised when the girl next to him began swaying and waving an arm to the rhythm, gripping the back of the pew with her other hand and jumping in on the chorus with unexpected enthusiasm. Up until then, Stu would have sworn she wasn't paying any attention. A minute later, it felt like the whole church began swaying, as the soloist reached a fervent crescendo. The air wafting up between all these bodies, all these raised arms in hot, close quarters, began to press on Stu with its pungent heft. He was about to sit when, at the minister's request, everyone around him began to sit down too.

The minister started his sermon in earnest and the pulsing cadence
of his speech lulled Stu back into his own thoughts. He had been to a lot
of funerals, those of his parents, Veronica's mom, his brother Matthew,
coworkers, and, now that he was teaching, a couple of students. His
parents had both died at this same time of year, the end of summer, three
years apart. The light cutting through the windows of Water of Life right
now had that same insistent, early autumn intensity he remembered
filling All Saints Lutheran during the services for his mother and father.

Veronica could laugh all she wanted, but Stu believed in funerals.
The culture was getting too casual, he told her. Funerals, with their
strict codes of behavior and dress, and rules for what you should say,
let you know there were still some standards. Showing up was important, so you could say to the family, "I was there. I was a witness to this
person's life." During the war he made it a point to be at every memorial
service or remembrance of his men that he could. If he couldn't be there,
he was religious about sending a condolence letter to the parents or wife
back home. He would take the time to tell the family his memories of
their soldier, even the soldiers he didn't particularly like. "You only die
once," he had said to Veronica on his way out the door that morning.
Whatever he thought of Johnquell's attitudes, he had known the kid.

The congregation was standing again. Another song, one he didn't
know. The girl next to him offered him a hymnal opened to the right
page but he just shook his head.

The thing about Johnquell's paper about Vietnam that ticked
Stu off the most was how he kept harping on the idea that all of the
MPs were white, as if blacks and Mexicans were being kept out on
purpose. If the kid hadn't stormed out of Stu's class, if he had ever come
back after that second day, Stu would have told him about Eddy
Wilson. Eddy was black and he was in the 721st MPs, too. There was
that other one, too, Parkman, but he got a mental health transfer out of
Long Binh after only a couple months, so maybe Parkman shouldn't
count.

Eddy was a solid guy, a good soldier and a good sport. Eddy sang in the Mountain Doo-Wops, this band he and a few other MPs put together. They used to play at the enlisted club and the occasional party, singing songs from Frankie Lymon and the Teenagers, and the Platters, with a little Beach Boys thrown in. Sometimes they got off key, but for Vietnam they were pretty good.

One time the band was going to play for the birthday of this MP named Frank Pancake. That was his real name. He said it was British. The other Doo-Wops thought it would be funny to dress up like Aunt Jemima, with head kerchiefs and blackface, the whole bit. They didn't tell Eddy, just showed up on the club stage like that.

"We're here for Pancake, get it?" Tony Moretti had said to Eddy, but Eddy didn't say anything, just led the Doo-Wops through a short set, wrapping up with "Happy Birthday." Eddy didn't stay for cake. He got a little moody sometimes.

Eddy was there for the riots Johnquell wrote his paper about, too, and he did his job as well as anybody. Stu would have told Johnquell about Eddy if he'd given him half a chance.

There was a rustling in the pews and a chorus of voices around him said, "Amen." The sermon was over. Now a bunch of students were lining up to talk at the mike.

"Excuse me," the girl next to Stu said. He stood up in the aisle to let her pass and watched her go up to the line.

A boy on stage was talking about Johnquell, about how they played on the varsity football team together. "Johnquell was a real team player," the boy was saying. "He was one of our best players, but whether we won or lost, it wasn't ever just about him. It was about the whole team."

The boy came down off the stage to applause. There were about twenty kids now in line to speak. It was going to be a while and he was pretty sure the funeral was about to devolve into some kind of group therapy session now that the students had the mike, so he decided to leave. Stu reached into the inner pocket of his coat where he had placed a thick envelope on his way out of the house. Inside it he had folded Johnquell's paper. He wanted the family to have it, since it was probably one of his last pieces of schoolwork, maybe the last. Stu had graded it— he gave it a C minus—since he expected to see Johnquell after their altercation, but the boy was absent from Stu's class for the rest of the semester. After Stu spoke to the attendance office about it, Johnquell's mother sent a note, excusing him for ten consecutive absences. The school let him graduate anyway. If Stu had been his regular teacher, he would have had something to say about that.

Stu had hesitated to bring the paper with him, since it was marked up. He had circled Johnquell's errors and written some commentary in the margins and at the end, including recommending a couple of books he might want to read. If the boy had come back he would have explained how strongly he felt that mistakes must be corrected. History is too easily manipulated if you let even the smallest misconception go. Look how Abraham Lincoln is portrayed in all the textbooks as the Great Emancipator, when in reality he was pro-slavery until it wasn't convenient anymore. Stu wondered sometimes if he had missed his calling. He might have made a difference in some young people's lives if he had chosen to become a history teacher instead of a corporate exec.

If Stu had known what was going to happen to Johnquell, of course he wouldn't have written anything on the paper, but this was a slice of the boy's real life. He thought the family would want to have it just the way it was. He wasn't sorry for the comments—they were true—but he did wish that it hadn't been necessary to mark it up with quite so much red.

He didn't know anybody in the family but the uncle to give it to, so he wrote on the outside of the envelope:

Leonard,

    I was the substitute teacher in Johnquell's Advanced U.S. History class for the last couple weeks of school. I thought the family might want to have this last paper he wrote for that class. After the incident on the street, I didn't think to give you this because I was thinking about the car of course.

Johnquell was a smart boy with a lot of potential. You have my deepest sympathies for your family's loss.

                                                            Stuart Reid

Stu thought that would be enough. Students were going up and down the aisle, to and from the stage. During the next outburst of applause, he made his way up to the front row, where he saw Leonard sitting with a woman with a face so afflicted and lost that Stu knew with one look that she was Johnquell's mother.

Leonard saw him and extended his hand. "Are you leaving?" Leonard had been crying and the whites of his eyes were streaked with red.

Stu bent in close to say, "Yes, I wanted to leave this with you though. It's some of Johnquell's schoolwork."

Beneath the applause and the sounds of crying, Leonard leaned into Johnquell's mother to say, "One of Johnquell's teachers." She looked up at Stu with interest and held out her hand, then withdrew it.

"You're the substitute," she said. Her voice was cold and scratchy.

"I'm very sorry . . . ," Stu began.

"I bet you are," she said, turning herself in the pew until she was facing the stage.

" . . . for your loss," Stu finished.

Leonard looked from Stu to Johnquell's mother and back again, but she kept her eyes on the stage.

"Thank you for coming," she said, without looking up.

Stu couldn't believe it. He hardly knew the boy but he had made the effort to be here, to honor her son's life, and she was dismissing him like a misbehaving student. He stood there a moment longer, but Johnquell's mother kept her eyes on the stage where three girls were getting ready to sing a song.

He turned away. Outside would be his battered car and the rest of a Saturday to do what he liked. As Stu made his way to the back of the church, he could hear one of the girls start up, her young voice strong enough to reach him even at the door.

Misdirected

On the sixth day after the funeral, Gloria stood up. She had tolerated the yellow carnations in the white wicker basket, with that ribbon stamped with parading geese, for just about too long.

Gloria picked up the basket from the lower shelf of the TV stand where her sister had stashed it. She pulled the tiny white envelope from the plastic spike that held it high over the heads of the flowers, like a messenger boy with an urgent telegram in some black-and-white movie.

"For Mother," it said in nun-trained script. Inside was a card, a background of soft-focus pink roses with a message written in the same hand: "Dear Mother, We're so glad to have found you. You were always in our hearts. Back soon. Love, Don and Paul."

When the basket had arrived in the days after the funeral, nobody thought too much about where they came from. Gloria's sister, Bee-Bee, simply signed the delivery receipt and shut the door. It seemed like just another offering in a house already too full of flowers—from friends of the family, relatives back in Mississippi who couldn't come up, a wreath that must have cost two hundred bucks from the teachers at the high school—and overflowing with food, all the foil-wrapped packages, angel food cakes, and plastic containers of potato salad people seem to think will make a woman feel better when she loses her first-born child.

Gloria had read the card before, but Don and Paul's carnations were just one more confusing thing in a sea of things that didn't make any sense. Now, though, with the relatives out of the house, the girls away at last-minute day camps that their neighbor Mrs. Czernicki arranged for them, and the minister not due to call until four o'clock, Gloria had a chance to consider what it said and to notice, for the first time, "Mother's" name and address printed on a label stuck to the back of the envelope.

"Huh," Gloria thought. "Donna Tillet of 2745 N. 65th St., meet Gloria Tibbetts of 2765 N. 45th St. Delivery man better get his glasses checked." She flicked the card down on the TV stand and went to sit back down on the couch, dropping to it with a force that made the imitation leather cushions wheeze. The beige couch had been her rock and refuge this first week, a boat on the sea where the girls could join her, curling around her and hiding their faces whenever one of the dozens of relatives tiptoeing around approached to quietly inquire whether anybody'd like a cup of tea or a little something to eat. But she was about done with all this sitting around. The empty house called to her now.

She went first to the kitchen. Besides the tower of scuffed and mismatched disposable containers pushed to one side of the green laminate counter, there wasn't even a spoon in sight. Every surface gleamed like it had been gone over twice with a toothbrush. Gloria had to stop and think when enough people had been in her kitchen long enough to get that accomplished. The days were fuzzy.

She climbed the stairs to the girls' bedrooms and peeked in the one at the front of the house that Raye-Raye and Nelly shared. It was spotless, too. The bright morning sun cast a glow on the girls' pink carpet. Normally, you couldn't see the floor, covered as it generally was with school papers, a jumble of clothes—clean and dirty—hair ties and brushes, and toys. Even Nelly's pony collection was lined up neatly on her white dresser and all of Raye's Lemony Snicket books were up on their shelf.

Neitha's room was smaller, darker, with only one north-facing window, but it also shone, cleaner and tidier than Gloria had ever seen it.

She felt a storm rise as she stood in Neitha's doorway, a surging wave of emotions—wonder at where her head was at while her relatives all had been so busy, a twinge of embarrassment at the exposure of every dusty cranny, and then a sweaty, voiceless rage at their stupid effort. None of it—not a swept floor, not a pile of clean dishes—was ever going to bring Johnquell back. The wave rose up and crested in a sudden, nauseated panic as she thought of him. Her breath caught and she bolted down the short hallway to the closed door at the end. She threw it open, letting it smack against the wall and shudder back toward her, and breathed a sigh of relief.

"Praise God," she said. The room was a wreck, with a week's worth of Johnquell's balled-up tube socks rolled into the corner, his bathrobe hanging on a nail he had punched into the wall next to his bed, and cords and dirty cups and candy wrappers strewn all over. The only suggestion of order was one she knew Johnquell had created himself: his supplies for college were arranged in three plastic crates and a couple sealed bins along the wall, ready for their journey to Madison. They had known to leave her this.

She sat on his bed and breathed in the boy-man smell of him. This room was a kind of portrait, of his carelessness, his fierceness, his dreams. She was never going to let anybody change it.

Gloria sat there on the bed for hours, his scent wrapping around her as it rose from the unwashed sheets. She sat, breathing, thinking, not crying. She had yet to really cry. She had wailed at the funeral, but even then no tears came, stopped up as they were with her disbelief. To let them run would be to let this impossible story out where it might get fixed as truth. She simply would not.

Gloria sensed the shadows make their rotation around the room in an unfocused way, until one edge crossed the face of Johnquell's alarm clock. She was startled to see that it was nearly one o'clock. Her mouth was dry and she felt a pang of hunger, a sensation she couldn't immediately identify. The feeling grew and became clearer, until she determined to get up and go look for some food in her bewildering, spotless kitchen.

She rose to her feet, unsteady on her stiff legs, and took in the room for a minute. There was a handprint on the white painted door frame, smudged but clearly the size and shape of Johnquell's hand. He must have put his football-player fingers in this same spot again and again passing through this door. Gloria pressed her face against the mark, feeling the cool wood on her cheek. She realized her eyes were wet. She wiped them with the edge of her sweatshirt, then she stepped over the threshold and closed the door behind her.

She ate her lunch in stages—a slice of slightly stale sheet cake, followed by a handful of potato chips, and then a plate of cold spaghetti with hot sauce—on the couch, each time walking from living room to kitchen and back with the same paper plate. The fourth trip was for one of the cans of Old Milwaukee someone—her brothers, Alston most likely—left in the fridge and the fifth trip was for another.

On the way back toward the couch she noticed the wilting carnations again and swiped the card off the TV stand. She stared at the tiny envelope for a good while, turning it over and over, reading first the handwritten "For Mother" on the front and then the computer-generated name and address on the back.

"Somebody's mother been missing her flowers," Gloria thought. Pulling the card out again, she read the puzzling message inside: "We're so glad to have found you."

"Huh," Gloria said out loud. "Or maybe somebody's mother just been plain missing."

※

When Gloria stepped out of the car in front of 2745 North Sixty-Fifth Street, the warm afternoon air against her skin was like a touch trying to rouse her out of a troubling dream. Gloria stood in the trim grass of the parkway for a minute and squeezed her eyes shut. How had she settled on this, making this trip twenty blocks to the neighborhood of Mrs. Donna Tillet with a basket of half-dead carnations? Maybe it was the beer. She considered getting back into the car, but by now the woman may have noticed her out there, a disoriented black woman in an all-white neighborhood. No. The best thing would be to follow through.

Gloria could feel the heat coming off the Tillets' dark green door and the evergreen hedges as she waited for someone to answer the bell. The spicy scent of the bushes wove into that of the carnations and wrapped itself around her head like a scarf. The sun off the windows glazed her eyes.

"Hello?" someone said. "Excuse me. Can I help you?"

For a moment, Gloria couldn't remember why she was here.

"Mrs. Tillet?" Gloria said, blinking at the short, white woman facing her through the screen door. She wore a yellow summer blouse that revealed her tanned arms and a pair of slim, dark jeans that seemed too young on this seventyish woman with clipped gray hair. "I think these were meant for you," Gloria said, holding out the basket.

Mrs. Tillet didn't take the basket right away. "Are you from the florist?" she asked.

"No," Gloria said. "These came to my house by mistake."

Mrs. Tillet reached out for the flowers then and looked them over. "When?" she asked, with a skeptical glance at their browning edges. "Not today."

Gloria had to think about it. She pressed her lips together and squinted her left eye in thought. "Well, let's see. The funeral was on Saturday and these came the next day, I think it was, so could it have been Sunday, maybe?" The reflected heat seemed to make the air around Mrs. Tillet's head waver. "Actually, I don't really know."

"I see," said Mrs. Tillet. She looked at the envelope on its spike and then up at Gloria and said, "Do you want to come in out of the sun and sit down for a minute? You look a little unsteady there."

It was cool inside the house. Gloria followed as Mrs. Tillet carried the basket to the dining room, just off the clay-tiled foyer, and set it in the middle of a blond oak dining table.

"Have a seat," Mrs. Tillet said, gesturing to one of the matching chairs. When Gloria didn't sit down right away, she gestured again. "Please," she said and went to the kitchen.

Gloria could hear her opening and closing the refrigerator and then pouring something.

"It's iced tea," Mrs. Tillet said, carrying in two tall glasses. "I hope that's alright. Do you want sugar?"

Gloria nodded and Mrs. Tillet went back for the sugar bowl and a spoon. The room was done up all country cute, with gingham curtains and antique blue enamel coffee pots. Don and Paul made a good call on the goose-ribbon and wicker basket.

When Mrs. Tillet had settled in, Gloria watched as she put on her reading glasses and read the small card. "Oh, how nice," Mrs. Tillet said. She leaned in to smell the carnations. "So sweet."

Gloria drank some of her tea. It was cold and gave Gloria brain freeze. An icy pain worked its way up her jaw and into her brow and scalp. She squeezed her eyes shut hard, until tears came to the edges but didn't quite fall.

"Are you OK?" Mrs. Tillet asked, putting a hand on Gloria's arm.

"I'll be fine in a minute," Gloria said.

When Gloria opened her eyes, the other woman was looking into her face. "You mentioned a funeral," Mrs. Tillet said. "Whose funeral, if I may ask?"

"My son." Gloria tried to say it like it was old news, but Mrs. Tillet reared back.

The room, with its bank of west-facing windows, seemed suddenly too bright. Gloria closed her eyes again.

"But you're so young. Are you forty even? How old could he have been?"

"Seventeen." Gloria opened her eyes.

"Just a baby. Oh, I am so sorry," Mrs. Tillet said. She had one hand over her mouth and the other back on Gloria's arm. "An accident or . . . ?"

"An accident. He was helping a neighbor and he fell." Gloria's voice cracked. She cleared her throat.

Mrs. Tillet said, "I am so, so sorry."

They sat looking at each other. A bird was outside the window chip-chipping, like it was counting.

"There was just so many flowers, you know? Just everywhere," Gloria said. "Then the delivery man came with these and, you know our names are close and so are the addresses, and I guess it's just, nobody really noticed he was in the wrong place until today."

Mrs. Tillet nodded. In the silence, Gloria's mind wandered back to the big spray of flowers on Johnquell's casket at the funeral. Leo had bought it, went all out for his nephew. Gloria had never seen so many lilies in one place, must have been a hundred.

Mrs. Tillet brought her back with a question, "Our names are close?"

"I'm Gloria Tibbetts. I'm at 2765 North Forty-Fifth."

"Oh," said Mrs. Tillet. "I see now." She glanced over at the carnations and then back at Gloria. "It's very nice of you to bring them by, with what all you must be dealing with and . . ." She trailed off, looking again into Gloria's face like she was searching for the answer to a question she couldn't quite articulate. "It really wasn't necessary."

Gloria straightened up in her chair. She had been slipping forward on the smooth, curved seat without noticing it. "I don't know. I'm a doer. I can't keep sitting in the house. I like to put things right. Feels like lots of things been lost lately and maybe this is one little thing I can put back where it belongs."

Mrs. Tillet nodded. "Of course."

"And anyway, you don't want to miss a note like that from your kids," Gloria said.

"No, you don't." Mrs. Tillet shook her head. "Well, it was very kind."

Gloria remembered the words on the card. "Were you lost, Mrs. Tillet?" she asked, taking a drink of her tea.

"I'm Donna. Call me Donna, please. And, no, I wasn't lost. I'm not sure what you mean."

Gloria wiped her mouth with her hand and pointed at the basket. "The flowers. The card says, 'We're so glad we found you.'"

"You read it?" Donna pushed a paper napkin toward Gloria across the narrow space that separated them. Her face clouded with anger for a moment and then cleared. "Oh, of course, you would have thought it was addressed to you. We're both 'Mother,' aren't we? Although . . . ," she started to say, a new note of confusion in her voice.

"I have other children," Gloria said.

Donna nodded. "Of course."

"Your children found you," Gloria said, hoping Donna would say more. It felt good to get into somebody else's business for a minute.

Donna put her hand over her mouth again and looked down at the table. "There is a story in that, isn't there?" Donna looked at Gloria out of the corners of her eyes.

Gloria nodded.

"Well, I guess I owe you an explanation, coming all this way just for the flowers." She pulled on the crux of her blouse, the place where the buttons started, almost like a man pulls to straighten his tie when he's nervous. "This is a bit strange. I'm a very private person. I wouldn't tell somebody about my personal business, particularly the first time I met them, normally."

"Donna, there ain't nothing normal about my life right now, nothing I'd recognize as such anyway," Gloria said. She whisked away a few drops of condensation from the table onto the floor and sat up straight again. She knew she looked formidable like that and something in this situation made her want to throw her weight around.

Donna nodded slowly, accepting the challenge. "Well, this is a strange time, for both us it seems." She paused. "One thing nobody mentions about getting older is, when you get to be my age you can sometimes run out of people to tell your stories to before you're done telling them. So, thank you, I guess.

"My sons, Don and Paul, were born in 1956 and '58. They're grown now, of course. Back in those days, a woman who, well." Donna stopped and took a drink of her tea. She coughed and said, "Maybe I should start at the other end.

"Don and Paul found me recently." Donna's voice sounded strained. "They found me again fifty years after their father took them away from me. He died—Parker, his name was—he died a couple years ago and that gave the boys the chance they needed finally to look me up."

"Hold on," Gloria couldn't help but ask, "you're saying that your grown children didn't talk to you for fifty years because their father didn't want them to?"

Gloria saw a flicker of doubt pass across Donna's eyes before she rolled her shoulders back and looked Gloria straight in the face. "That's what Don said and I'm inclined to believe him. Parker was a very forceful man and he had strong feelings about this sort of thing. He had a brother who, well, that's another story. I was talking about the boys."

Gloria shrugged. "OK."

"First they wrote and I wrote back. Then we had a few phone calls and e-mails and then last week, they came to see me." Her gray-blue eyes were filled with tears but she was smiling. "You can imagine what I thought, holding that first letter. I could hardly read it my hands were shaking. It's like they were reborn."

"Reborn," Gloria repeated.

"Yes, and they turned out so good. They grew up to be really good men, just solid, upstanding citizens. Donny is an insurance agent and Paulie is in the remodeling business. Donny got married and had three children, who are grown themselves. Paulie never did get married, but they all just turned out so well. My great-granddaughter sent me a picture. It's on the fridge." Donna seemed poised to spring up and go get the drawing but Gloria interrupted her.

"That's great," Gloria said, but she was thinking of Johnquell, how he wasn't going to become an insurance agent or get into the remodeling business or anything.

"They want to bring me out to California for Christmas and I told them I'd be there in a heartbeat, just say the word." Donna's face was glowing and she was leaning forward on the edge of her seat. "I mean, what's holding me here? Nothing." She opened her hands as if to show the emptiness of the room. "Nothing."

Gloria felt the loss of her child then like a hot iron rod through her chest. She could almost hear the searing of her flesh, the singeing of the ragged edges of the wound. Johnquell, her son, wasn't ever going to fly her out to California to show her his fancy, paid-up house and her beautiful, smiling grandkids with their straight, white teeth and their Xbox or Nintendo or whatever they're all going to have by then. There wasn't ever going to be any Fourth of July barbecues on the patio, no promotions at work, no smiling at her Johnquell across the room at Christmas and knowing, knowing without saying anything, she made that.

"Are you OK?" Donna was asking. "Here's me, prattling on and on. You'll have to excuse me," she said, but she didn't sound like she wanted to be excused for anything. Her face was beaming, like every weight of a lifetime had been lifted, and she looked twenty years younger than when Gloria first saw her half an hour ago.

Gloria wanted to smack her.

"Why'd they take your kids away?" Gloria asked. The question cut Donna's mood as quick as someone pulling the plug on the DJ at a dance.

Donna sat back in her seat. "Oh, I don't think you want to hear about that."

"Yeah, I do," Gloria said. She said it in that tone of voice she used with the deadbeat dads in her job at the county child support enforcement office, maternal concern backed by the heavy hand of state authority. "I want to know all about it."

Donna looked Gloria in the eyes and Gloria could see something different there now, a mix of sadness and a sober sort of fear. She heard Donna swallow hard before she began to speak.

"You have to remember it was the early '60s. I know you probably weren't even born yet, but I'm sure you've heard stories about that time, how bad it was, for your people."

Gloria rolled her eyes. Nice white people like to remind you how bad the bad old days were. What they generally forget to mention is that it's still bad.

"I mean, for anyone who was different from the mainstream, really. I was married, got married in 1955, because I had to. We caught it early and got married quick, so I wasn't even showing when we had our wedding. I don't know that I could say I was in love with Parker but he was smart and strong. I didn't know what I wanted out of life, but Parker seemed to, and that was very attractive."

Gloria asked, "He knew what he wanted out of life or he knew what you wanted out of life?" The cold tea had finally washed away the fuzz of the beer and the day's heat.

"At the time, I was pretty sure he would figure it out for the both of us." Donna shook her head and laughed. "I was a fool. He didn't have a clue what I wanted."

"What did you want?" Gloria asked, but she had a couple ideas. She had just noticed a picture on the wall behind Donna's head. It had taken a while for Gloria's eyes to focus on it, but now she could clearly see that it was a picture of a younger Donna, in a royal blue sweater and long, black skirt that would have been in style in the '80s, sitting in an armchair. A dark-haired woman stood behind her, with a hand on each shoulder, as if keeping Donna turned to the camera. Not a real strict pose like you would do at a studio, but close enough. A family picture.

"I had a friend, a woman," Donna said.

"Her?" Gloria asked, pointing toward the picture on the wall.

Donna turned to look. "No. Not her." Donna winced like something pinched her. "I'm talking about my friend Myrna. She and I were close, so close that Parker began to get jealous of the time we spent together. One time—the year Donny was going on six—we had a New Year's Eve party and invited a bunch of the neighbors. Parker was in a temper and he was following me and Myrna around the house all night. It was making me angry and I guess we were being careless, but he saw us in the kitchen, holding hands while we were in there pretending to get more ice."

"You were in love with her?" Gloria asked, even though she could see the answer all over Donna's face.

"Yes, I think I was." Donna nodded. Funny as it seemed to Gloria that two women could love each other the same way a man and a woman could, anybody could see it was still the same look.

"What happened after he saw you?"

"At first, nothing. He didn't speak to me, just stormed off."

"And?"

"This is ugly. I'm sorry, what he did next is just ugly. I don't like to say."

"Life can get ugly," Gloria said.

Donna reached out and put a hand over Gloria's. "God, yes. Of course you know that." She met Gloria's eyes and then picked up her glass and looked into it a moment before taking a drink. Her voice was quieter when she started up again. "Parker got so drunk that after the midnight toasts and 'Auld Lang Syne' and all that, he called out to everyone, saying, 'Wait. Wait just a second. I have one more thing to say. My wife . . .'" Donna held out her tea like it was a champagne glass and waved it with the unsteady movement of a drunken man. "'My wife is a no-good whore. I just thought you should know. So happy new year everybody,' and he raised his glass toward me like he was toasting me."

Gloria shook her head. "King of ugly."

Donna nodded. She picked up her napkin and began folding it into a triangle, turning it, unfolding it, and starting over. "At first I couldn't move. I heard the neighbors talking but I couldn't make out the words. The sounds all blended together and I must have fainted because next thing I know, I'm propped up on the powder room toilet and Marcelline Anderson is wiping my face with a cold washcloth. I asked her, 'Where's Myrna?' and I will remember the look Marcelline gave me, deep in my eyes, for the rest of my life; she said, 'I think that ought to be the least of your worries, where Myrna is.' Marcelline had my hair in her big hand and she gave my head a good tug, like you would to a child you were trying to get in line, and she said, 'If I were you, I wouldn't say that name again for a long time and I'd get up early tomorrow morning and clean up this house and fix your hair and make your husband a nice dinner. And I don't think anybody should have to say another word about it.'"

Donna shook the ice cubes in her nearly empty glass, spinning them around like someone at a bar wondering whether to order another.

"Whole neighborhood closed ranks on you, huh?" Gloria said. "That's hard."

"It was hard, but the harder part came later. I tried to be a good wife, tried to keep from calling Myrna, visiting her. Myrna tried too, but we couldn't stay away. Finally, Myrna's husband took a job in Atlanta and they moved. That was the only thing that kept us apart."

"Did you ever see her again?" Gloria asked.

"No. We didn't even write. Didn't dare." Donna's voice grew quiet.

"I met this other woman, Joyce, about a year later at a gardening club I started going to to keep my mind occupied. I could tell Joyce was different, too. She was in her thirties but she wasn't married, said she had no intention of ever getting married. She was a career woman. One time she invited me out for a drink. Parker was out of town for something for work and so I got a babysitter and Joyce picked me up. We went to this place on the edge of downtown, the River Boat. I was twenty-six years old, lived here all my life, and had never heard of it. Turns out it was a gay bar. I didn't even know we had those in Milwaukee."

"Really?" Gloria asked. For a lesbian, it seemed like Mrs. Donna Tillet had a pretty picture of herself, Gloria thought, all Sunday-going-to-meeting.

"Really," Donna said. "I mean, we weren't raised to even consider such a possibility. Things were different then." She waited to go on until Gloria gave her a nod. "I got the once-over from every woman in that bar, let me tell you. I could hardly breathe with them looking at me. There were men there too and even a few drag queens. I have no idea what Joyce and I talked about because I was scared out of my wits, but still, once I could take a real look around I felt this relief wash over me, knowing that there were others like me. This is going to sound crazy, but sitting there on that stool, trembling like a bird, I had this vision of a door opening onto something I couldn't see but that I knew was better than the way I had lived so far.

"Have you ever felt like that?" Donna asked.

Gloria shook her head. "No, can't say I have."

It wasn't "can't" so much as "don't want to." She could have told Donna about how she felt when she decided to leave her own snake of a husband, or about the day she enrolled in the BA program even though she didn't know how she was going to pay for it. She knew all about that feeling but she wasn't exactly in the mood for swapping starting-over stories. Not now.

"Well, anyway. The sense of relief lasted all of about ten minutes because next thing I know, both the back and front doors of the bar fly open and a dozen cops run in with their billy clubs and chase me and everybody else off the bar stools and into wagons waiting in the alley.

"I got charged with 'indecent public behavior' or something like that. All of our names were in the paper the next day. The couple of us married women were listed by the husbands' names, so I guess it was kind of a rude shock to my husband to know the neighbors could read about 'Mrs. Parker Tillet' at every newsstand in town.

"The day after that, Parker came home with divorce papers. He told me, 'Better get yourself a good lawyer and a way to pay him.' I left after that, packed up a little bag—left everything, the kids' drawings in the hallway, my mom's wedding jewelry, my birth certificate, all of it—and called Joyce. I didn't know where else to go." Donna began to cry, quiet tears that made their way down her powdered, tanned face and dropped onto her shirt.

"Parker got the boys. His lawyer fought hard, threw every accusation at me that he thought might stick. Several neighbors who I thought were my friends came to testify against me, about how they had seen me with Myrna." Donna closed her eyes for a few seconds. "Marcelline, too. Just put it all out there, things I didn't even know anybody had noticed, like this little heart charm I had bought Myrna for her charm bracelet. Parker got the boys and he took them to California and cut off all contact. It was like they had died, except I knew that they were still alive."

Gloria felt Donna's words like smack on the head and she moved in her chair like she had been hit.

"Oh, I'm sorry," Donna said. "That was insensitive."

Gloria waved the apology away. She wanted to feel that right now, the still-alive feeling. She wanted to feel it so bad that Johnquell was in the room with them for just a minute. Gloria tried to focus on it, to hold him there, but he got away. That feeling had come and gone over the days since he passed. It was getting fainter, harder to grasp.

When Gloria tuned back in, Donna was going on. "For a lot of years, I got kind of lost in self-pity," she was saying. "Self-hatred, I guess. I lived with Joyce and we drank too much and I didn't have the heart to find the boys. I couldn't imagine how their life would be better with a drunk dyke of a mother in it—that's how I thought of myself then, drunk dyke. Whenever I thought of it I just drank more, so I just stopped thinking. I just moved on as best I could.

"I could see them, in my mind's eye, in California. Like I was floating above them. Somehow I always imagined them running around on a big green lawn, running through a sprinkler and laughing. They always stayed the same ages, six and eight, the ages when they left."

"And now they're back," Gloria said, finishing Donna's story for her.

"And now they're back," Donna said.

They sat there, not talking, while the condensation on the chilled glasses made water rings on the oak table, until the clock in the foyer rang four times.

"The minister," Gloria said, standing up.

"What?"

"Pastor Thomas. He's coming by my house right about now. I should go." Gloria wasn't looking forward to his visit. Somehow he always managed to make everything about him.

"Oh," Donna said. "Yes, by all means, go see him." She pulled herself up too, the age returning to her body.

Back outside, the spell of their conversation was broken and they stood, Gloria on the sidewalk and Donna on the steps.

Finally, Donna said, "This has been strange." She squinted into the bright sunlight where Gloria stood. "Good, but strange."

"Yeah, I came to bring the flowers and then, yeah. Strange," Gloria said, looking toward the car where it sat, cool and dark, underneath the shade of a tall elm. The thought of getting into it and driving back to the childless house scared her, and Pastor Thomas would be cold comfort. She turned back and said, "Can I ask you one more thing?"

"At this point, I guess you could ask me anything," Donna said. Her face had softened, all the tension of admitting the story of her past gone.

"What happened with you and Joyce?"

"Oh, we managed to stay together, a long time. She died three years ago."

Gloria's throat felt dry and tight. She coughed and found enough voice to say, "I'm sorry to hear that."

"Yes. And I'm sorry, dear. I'm sorry for your loss, too." Donna's voice faltered. "Words seem so inadequate at times like these," she said.

Gloria said, "His name was Johnquell."

"Johnquell," Donna repeated and stepped out onto the walkway. She held out her arms and Gloria walked into them and cried.

That's the Way Cats Are

Frances always put her keys in the brown ceramic bowl on the little table in the foyer. The clatter of metal hitting clay told her she was home, a message that echoed up the high wooden staircase. Bean, the cat, would come down, stretching her white toes and stout, gray legs along the way and mewing hello.

"Is it time?" Frances would ask and Bean would tell her it was by slinking past her to the kitchen, then waiting by her bowl near the dishwasher. The bowl said "Bean" on it. It was a gift from Frances's brother, Theo, and it had arrived from some mail-order house a couple of weeks after Frances brought Bean home from the Humane Society. Why the cat needed a personalized food dish, she would never know. It's not like the animal could read. Theo was like that, always wasting money on gifts.

But maybe Theo was right to try to spoil the creature a little bit. After all, Bean had been Frances's only companion in the big foursquare house since Chester died. The cat could be trouble, though, shedding on everything, scratching the fine old Arts and Crafts woodwork, and even bringing half-dead mice up from the basement like trophies to share with Frances.

It was Bean who got Frances into some of the most painful trouble of her seventy-five years. Late one September night, Frances had been awakened as usual by the need to use the toilet. On her way back, she tripped over the cat. As Frances fell, she felt her right knee twist and a sharp pain as she hit the floor. Still, she managed to hobble back to bed.

In the morning she was surprised to find her knee was swollen so badly she couldn't bend her leg. She slid it over the edge of the bed and it thumped on the carpet like a log, sending a rattling sting all through her body. Frances thought the better of standing on it and instead called her brother.

"Theo, I hurt my damn knee. I don't think I can drive. Come take me to the doctor, will ya?"

"I'm at the grocery store right now," he said. Theo had a cell phone. Frances never knew where he was going to be when she called. "If I can put my ice cream in your freezer when I get there, I'll just come now."

"Just come, OK?" she said. Theo and his ice cream. Sometimes that's all he'd eat for dinner, like he was six instead of sixty-five. Still, he was a skinny thing for all the butter pecan he put away. He reminded his sister of a cotton swab, with his thick, white tuft of hair on top of that lanky body. Frances was thin, too, shorter than Theo but strong for her age. She hated having to call on him for help on things like this.

As soon as she hung up the phone, she started pulling on some pants, a T-shirt, and a Packers sweatshirt she found at the top of the hamper near the bed. She didn't bother with shoes, just put her slippers on. The effort of getting dressed had her grunting and biting her tongue, and she was sweating and crankier than a badger by the time Theo let himself in.

"What took you so long?" Frances asked when Theo appeared in the doorway of her room.

Theo looked at the watch on his bony wrist. "That was eleven minutes. I got here as quickly as I could. Should I go?" He could get like that, all high and mighty, if you crossed him.

Frances glared at him. "Call Dr. Matthews and find out if he can see me."

Theo picked up the phone and called, smirking a little as he did. Frances heard him ask the receptionist if there were any appointments available this morning, then he put the receiver on his shoulder and said, "He's out today. Do you want to make one for tomorrow?"

"No," Frances snapped.

He told the receptionist, "We'll try urgent care. Thank you."

Frances didn't like urgent care, the medical world's equivalent of Siberia. Doctors stationed there were isolated, exiled for untold crimes, she thought. You never knew if your test results would get to your regular doctor's office and so half the time you had to take the same tests there too, and you got double the poking and prodding. Plus all the urgent care doctors were women named "Chelsea" or "Kaitlyn" or, worse, were Indian, with funny last names that Frances would spend the entire visit trying to sound out off the badges on their white coats.

Getting Frances down the stairs was a project. Bean thought that for sure Frances was coming downstairs to feed her and stayed close and underfoot, keeping an eye on the clumsy procession until finally Theo yelled, "Get, Bean!" She skittered down the rest of the stairs and disappeared in the direction of the kitchen.

At the front door Frances said, "Wait, Theo," putting a hand on his forearm. "Go give Bean some food before we go. You never know how long they're going to make you wait at those damn places."

"Can you stand that long?" Theo asked, looking her up and down as he let go.

"Yeah, I'm fine. Just go feed her already." Frances gestured toward the kitchen with her left hand and steadied herself with her right on the wall. She rubbed the top of the entryway's dark wainscot while she waited, trying to keep her mind off her knee. Little balls of dust worked up under her fingers and she flicked them away. She should get someone in here to help her clean, she thought, but it was hard to trust people these days.

She could hear Theo in the kitchen at the other end of the house, talking to Bean in a high-pitched voice that she would have found embarrassing if they weren't alone. When Theo returned they made their way to his old Volvo and he helped her in. As they took off down Montana Street she asked, "Why do you talk to her like that?"

"Talk to who like what?"

"Like, 'And are we ready for some food? Oh, yes we are. We love our food, don't we?'" Frances said, mimicking Theo's trembly sing-song. "I mean, she's not a baby. She's a cat—a six-year-old cat. That's an adult in cat years, a mature woman. Do you talk to mature women like that?"

"I don't know any mature women, except you," Theo said, keeping his eyes on the road. The car hit a pothole and Frances's leg flew up a bit, her heel hitting the floor of the car on the way back down.

"Ah!" Frances cried, leaning over to slide her hands between the seat and her knee. "Careful!"

"Of course," said Theo.

They were heading up Forest Home Avenue, right next to the cemetery. "Pabst, Schlitz, and Blatzes, Forest Home is where it's at-zes," Theo sang. It was a stupid song he made up for a history skit when he was in sixth grade. He looked over at Frances. "Your line."

"Titans of beer, sausage, and leather. All of them dead together," Frances grumbled. "Really, Theo, I'm not in the mood."

The urgent care clinic was located in an ugly little strip mall on Lincoln Avenue. Frances remembered the pharmacy that used to be there. Dalton's Drugs. They bulldozed Dalton's ten years before, a glossy white-tiled building with painted terra cotta flowers in baskets all along the top. She used to sit out there in the car while Chester went inside to get their prescriptions filled and, to pass the time, imagine plucking the flowers out one by one and letting them fall onto the sidewalk.

Once inside the clinic, Frances and Theo had to wait for half an hour. A young mother had come in just before them, with a rosy-faced, screaming toddler.

"Ear infection," the mother said to Frances and Theo apologetically as she sat down as far away as possible. In the compact room, that wasn't all that far.

"Whatcha got there, little guy?" asked Theo, gesturing at the yellow flannel bundle the kid had pressed to the side of his head. "Is that a rabbit?"

The kid just wailed more loudly. Frances was surprised Theo even tried. Normally he hated children. Maybe the screaming snapped some nerve in his head. He looked at Frances and shrugged.

A woman with a taut bandage over her forearm emerged from the exam rooms. She looked sticky and pale, her curly hair matted around her face with sweat or water.

"What will you do about the dogs?" the receptionist asked from behind the desk. "Do you need me to call someone for you?"

"Oh, no," said the woman with the bandage. "I can get them back home. It's only a few more blocks and they won't give me any more trouble. I think they're pretty embarrassed by the whole thing."

The woman left and Frances could hear the receptionist say to a nurse in pink scrubs, "An embarrassed dog? I thought the whole point of being a dog was that you never had to be embarrassed."

"That would explain the mastiffs outside," Theo said. There had been two enormous dogs with mottled black and brown coats, one tied to the railing on either side of the ramped entryway, when they came in.

"And I thought they were just a sign that we were crossing over the river into hell," said Frances.

A few minutes later the nurse in pink scrubs poked her head out from behind a door near the receptionist's desk and called for the screaming toddler—Ethan—and his mom. They followed the nurse and when the kid's cries had been muffled by the closing door and some distance, Frances looked at Theo and said, "Thank God."

Theo just shrugged. He was working the crossword puzzle. "What's a seven-letter word for 'impatient'?"

Frances shifted in her chair and winced at the pain in her knee. "How should I know?"

"Frances?" called the nurse, appearing again at the door.

"That's me," said Frances, pushing herself up with both arms before Theo could set down his newspaper. Theo grabbed her right elbow and helped her toward the door.

"How are we doing, Frances?" the nurse asked, with a business-like smile.

"We'll be doing a lot better just as soon as we can see the doctor," said Frances, grimacing with each step down the short hallway to the exam room.

"Dr. M. will be in to see you in just a minute," the nurse said after directing Frances and Theo to chairs along the wall of the all-white room. They sat facing the same direction, not talking or looking at each other, Frances emitting a sigh now and then as she watched the clock.

"Urgent, my ass," Frances said.

After about fifteen minutes, there was a rap of knuckles at the door, making them both jump. Before they could collect themselves to answer, a woman with a blonde ponytail and a white lab coat strode in. "Hello, Mrs. Clark. I'm Dr. M.," she said, looking at the paper stapled to the manila folder she carried while reaching out to shake Frances's hand. As the doctor leaned in, Frances read her name tag. It said, "B. Muthukumarasamy, MD."

"You're kidding me," Frances hissed.

"I'm sorry?" Dr. M. said, smiling vaguely.

"Nothing," said Frances.

The doctor and Theo introduced themselves and then helped Frances up to the exam table. Dr. M. looked to be in her early thirties, with a few lines around her mouth that would grow into real wrinkles soon, Frances thought.

The doctor pressed on different parts of Frances's leg, asking, "Is this tender? Here? Here?" until she hit a spot on the inner knee and Frances gasped. "Tender?" Dr. M. asked then, studying Frances's face.

"That's not the word I would use," Frances said, clenching her teeth.

"Looks like an MCL sprain, Mrs. Clark. We can do an X-ray to see how bad it is, but the recommendation at this point will probably be the same regardless: resting with the leg up and braced, ice, medication, and time."

"How much time?"

"Depends on your body. Could be a couple of weeks or a couple of months."

"Months? My leg is going to be like this for months?"

"It could be. The older you are the longer it can take. But the sooner you start treating it the better. And when you see your regular doctor you might want to get a referral for a physical therapist, to help you strengthen the area around the injury, once you can walk again."

"Once I can walk again? I just tripped over the damn cat. I'm not disabled." Frances turned her head to see what Theo was making of this, but he just lifted both his hands in a silent "Who knows?"

"Talk with your doctor," Dr. M. said. She wrote a quick note and snapped her pen back onto her coat pocket. "In the meantime, unless you feel strongly about it, I'm not going to do an X-ray at this point. It's not likely to tell us anything more than what we already know. Your regular doctor is probably going to want to follow up with some pictures, though, once we get some of that swelling down, OK?" Frances nodded and Dr. M. went on, "I'm going to send the nurse in with a brace and a set of crutches, and . . ."

"I don't need them," Frances said.

"Don't need what?" Dr. M. asked.

"The crutches. I have some already." There was a set in the basement from when Chester was alive.

"You have them here?" Dr. M. asked, looking around.

"No. At home."

"Well, I need you to leave here with the most protection possible for that knee, so I'm going to have Lisa bring them in and . . ." In spite of Frances's challenge, Dr. M.'s face was set with another one of those vague smiles.

They must have a whole class on meaningless facial expressions in medical school, Frances thought. She said, "How much are they going to cost?"

"Cost? I don't know, but the important thing is to get any possibility of weight off of that knee."

"No, the important thing is that I pay the electric bill on the thirtieth."

"Frances," said Theo, in a voice that sounded surprisingly like their mother's. "Don't be so difficult. She's only trying to help you."

Frances was still on her back, hands folded over her belly and eyes looking up at the flat fluorescent panels in the acoustic tile ceiling. Her entire body was tense and still except for the sharp line of fire that ran through her knee and out her mouth.

"What's difficult is paying for all this crap they try to load you down with, like it's a shopping spree at Boston Store or something."

Dr. M. sighed. "Fine, I'll send Lisa in with a brace and the crutches, and you can decide to take what you want. If you don't take the crutches you're going to have to sign an AMA waiver saying that you're going against doctor's advice. She'll also give you a care instruction sheet with a phone number on it. Call the desk with any questions, OK? Take good care." Dr. M. gave Frances a dismissive pat on her folded hands.

"That's it?" Frances let out a disbelieving puff of air. "Wait a minute," said Frances, raising herself up on her elbows. Theo jumped up to help her sit up on the table.

Dr. M. turned back. "Yes?"

"How do you say your name?"

"Brittney?" Dr. M. said with a half-cocked smile.

"No, the other one."

"Oh. Moo-took-koo-mah-rah-sah-mee. My husband's Indian. People pretty much just call me 'Dr. M.' OK, take care now." The door clicked shut behind her and a second later Frances heard her calling to someone in the hall.

Lisa came in shortly, with the threatened brace, crutches, and paperwork in hand. "Believe me, you're gonna want these, too," she said of the crutches, after Frances consented to the brace. They were still wrapped in a long plastic bag, gray metal with molded hand grips, almost athletic looking. In fact, the royal blue foam caps and grips reminded her of the color of racquet balls. Chester used to play that, at the Y.

"No," Frances said to the nurse. "I have some already."

Frances signed the paperwork and they left, the brace on her leg and the information sheet in hand.

"That wasn't too bad, now was it?" Theo said when they were back in the car.

"What part? The screeching toddler? The $150 worth of Velcro I've got on my knee? Dr. Brittney who probably graduated from medical school last week? At least the dogs were off duty by the time we left, or I might not have gotten out alive." Her whole body was steaming with rage.

"You're going to be fine, Frances," Theo said, ignoring her and pulling out of the parking lot.

"Of course I'm going to be fine. Did I say anything about not being fine? I probably won't be when I see the final bill, but for now, I'm fine. OK?"

Theo looked at her out of the corner of his eye and tightened his lips into a thin line. "OK. You're fine. What do you want for lunch?" They were passing a taco truck parked on the shoulder on Forty-Third Street. "Burrito?"

"Are you kidding? Just take me home. I'll fix myself something there."

But she couldn't, once they got back to her house. With Theo's help, Frances got up the front steps and made it as far as the couch in the living room before collapsing. She sat there and stared out the window. Her leg was a tower of pain. The instruction sheet said she was supposed to keep it elevated, so Theo helped her position it among some pillows he placed on the coffee table.

Then he made himself useful, getting her painkillers, offering her a magazine, which she refused. He made them each a cheese sandwich and heated up some tomato soup, bringing it out on a tray. Bean came to sit by Frances, first smelling the brace up and down and finally curling up on the couch with her solid spine pressed into Frances's hip. Frances made a point of shifting now and then to force Bean to get up and re-organize herself. "Damn cat."

They ate without speaking. Theo looked around the room in between bites, and Frances watched him, following his gaze from the Morris chair with the rip in the brown leather to the green chinaberry-pattern rug, worn down to gray along the edges. His attention caught on a place up near the ceiling where a piece of the pinstriped wallpaper was peeling back. Frances had meant to get to that, paste it back down.

When he was halfway done with his sandwich, Theo said, "Frances, I was thinking."

"Uh-oh. Stand back, world!" she said.

"Ha-ha. But seriously, I was thinking that maybe it's time to sell this big house. I mean, sitting here today I can really feel how big and empty it is now that Chester is gone."

"Now that he's gone? He's been gone for ten years. You just noticed that he's gone? He was quiet but he wasn't that quiet."

"No, I mean, isn't it time you thought about downsizing?" He waved an arm toward the empty wood-paneled dining room. "You don't need all this space and it's got to be hard for you to take care of it all, the dusting, the vacuuming, shoveling in the winter."

"Well, things are easier now that I've given up shoveling in the summer." Frances pursed her lips and then took a prim bite of her sandwich.

"Just stop, alright? And listen? Have you ever seen the apartments at the Protestant Home, on the east side? Bill Rumford lives there. It's nice." Theo's gray eyes lit up with enthusiasm.

"I'm not a Protestant, remember?" Frances had converted to Catholicism years ago, a condition of her marriage. Her Lutheran mother could hardly bring herself to attend the wedding at St. Sebastian's, Chester's family's church.

"Well, then the Catholic Home, or what have you. Does it really matter?"

"Are you serious? You're going to bring this up now?" She glared at him. "You probably think you can pull one over on me while I'm in some kind of weakened state, but we settled this already. I'm not like you, you know. I need space to move around in. I don't like apartments. They feel fake, like you're a kid just playing at living. Like you're in a doll house."

"But it would make things so much easier."

"Easier for who? For you? Am I that much trouble? It's not like I ask for your help that much. When's the last time I asked you for help?"

"You mean, like this morning?" Theo arched an eyebrow.

"That was an accident. It could happen to anybody. I mean before that."

"Well, on Saturday you asked me to change that lightbulb in the hall closet." The smug look on his face made Frances furious.

"And is that such a big deal? Changing a lightbulb?"

"That's not the point, Frances. It's more than that."

Frances followed his deliberate look back at the peeling wallpaper but she stayed on the attack. "Don't you dare tell me that you worry about me here alone," she said, scanning his face for clues about what he was up to. "That's what everybody says when they're trying to get some old biddy off to the nursing home. 'You don't want to make us worry, do you?' and next thing you know her appliances are sold off and she's got her nose pressed to the passenger-side window of the U-Haul. No, you don't need to worry about me. I walk, I drive, I do my own grocery shopping. I can remember what year it is, who's president, and which pills I take on what day. I've been fine here alone for ten years and I expect I can do ten more." Frances threw the crust of her sandwich down and flashed Theo a challenging look. For a minute, she forgot about the pain in her knee.

"Frances, I'm not talking about a nursing home. I'm talking about a smaller place, that's all, one that's easier to take care of and where there are other people around the clock."

"Well, you can stop talking about it, because I'm not going anywhere."

They finished their lunch in silence. Before Theo left, Frances sent him into the basement to find the old set of crutches that she knew were still down there somewhere, from when Chester had sprained his ankle years ago. Frances remembered the year—1976—because getting down to their customary spot by the lake for watching the fireworks was a lot harder, what with the oversized crowd for the Bicentennial and Chester's crutches. He hurt himself just the Saturday before, running after a Frisbee in the parkway. Some kids were throwing one around and he stupidly asked if he could join in. He was still a kid inside, even at almost fifty. Maybe it was because they could never have children of their own, but he never quite grew up, never got old until the very end. He liked kids, though, liked their energy. Frances could always take 'em or leave 'em. Just a lot of mess and trouble.

Theo brought up the crutches and leaned them up against the arm of the couch.

"Anything else?" he asked, wiping his hands on his brown wool pants.

"Huh?" Frances was startled out of that memory, Chester on the parkway with those kids. She missed him, the way he could coax her out into the world with his silly notions about what constituted a good time. Those Frisbee kids would all be grown now, in their forties, doing their own foolish things, thinking they were still young.

"I said, did you need anything else?" Theo repeated.

It took Frances a second to focus on his face. "No. I'm fine."

"What are you going to do tonight?" he asked.

"What do you mean?"

"How are you going to get up the stairs?"

"I'll figure something out. Can't stay down here all the time."

Theo stood there a minute, his hand on his hip. Finally, Frances said, "I'll be fine," wrinkling her nose at him like he smelled bad, a gesture left over from childhood. "Go already."

She spent the afternoon on the couch, watching old movies on cable. Sometime in the middle of *Key Largo* the phone rang but Frances didn't even try to answer it. She heard the answering machine beep but couldn't make out the voice. Whatever. She nodded off. It was dark when she woke to Bean's insistent demand for attention. The cat was alternating between meowing and tapping Frances on the cheek and forehead with her damp nose. The glowing numbers on the side table clock read 8:37.

"Oh, Bean. I'm sorry. Let me just get up and I'll get you your food." Frances pressed her hands to her face, trying to wipe away the fatigue she felt at the thought of making her way across the house. She pulled the cord on the lamp on the end table and slid her heavy leg off the couch. She put on her glasses and gave herself a minute to get used to sitting up. As the blood flowed back into her leg she felt a sickening pain. It reminded her to take one of the pain killers Theo had dutifully left with a small glass of apple juice on the end table. Her mouth had dried out while she slept and her tongue felt like the flap door on an old canvas tent, but the juice was soothing and the chalky pill went down fine.

She gripped the pads of the crutches and noticed that they had hardened over the years. They were tough and discolored, hardly cushions now. A piece of foam had chipped off of one of the pads, leaving a powdery hole shaped like the imprint of a brain. She stood and fixed one crutch into each armpit, gingerly shifting her weight onto her hands. She knew that you're supposed to keep your weight on your hands, not under your arms. "Easier said than done," Frances thought to herself after only a few awkward steps. She made a side trip to the bathroom and by the time she fumbled her way into the kitchen the skin under her armpits felt burnt and overextended, like an old elastic waistband.

Frances slid the plastic tub of cat food from its place on the counter near the toaster. As long as she squeezed the crutches with her upper arms, she could pivot in a tight half circle, but she couldn't bend over to get closer to the bowl. She took the measuring cup and poured the cat food from standing height. The hard bits fell everywhere, half in and half out of the bowl. Bean looked up at her indignantly.

"Too bad," Frances said. "It'll taste just as good off the tile as it does in the bowl. It's your fault I can't get down there anyhow." She worried briefly about mice or roaches but only briefly. She was too tired to care.

Maneuvering herself to the cabinet that held the glasses, she got a tumbler from the lowest shelf and filled it with water. When she had drained the glass, she put it in the pocket of her slacks and went out to the dining room. In the built-in china cabinet there wasn't any china, but there was a bottle of scotch that had Frances's name on it, literally. Hanging on a silver chain over the neck of the bottle was a small gleaming plaque with "Frances" etched in script. Another stupid gift from Theo. "I know how much you like your nightcap," he had said as she pulled the plaque from its tissue paper bed. "Now everyone will know the bottle is yours."

"Everyone" being who? she had wondered. Chester was more of a beer kind of guy. Peppermint schnapps if the moment called for it, maybe, but he had never been tempted to drink her whisky. The dainty plaque did cast a certain feminine shine on her habit, though, like a charm bracelet on a big-boned woman's wrist. She kept it, moved it from empty bottle to full before throwing the empty into the trash.

She opened the stained glass door of the built-in with a tug. She reached into the familiar recess of the cabinet, the scent of old gin and long-ago parties drifting up to her nose, and gripped the bottle. She poured herself a good measure into the tumbler. By the time Frances had the scotch in hand, Bean had finished her scattered meal and came out into the dining room, licking her lips and looking askance at Frances as she walked by.

"What, cat? You're not grateful?" Frances called after her. "It was still food, you know, which is more than I'm going to get." But Bean was ignoring her and had already wandered off into some other room, no doubt to rest after the exertions of hunting and pecking for her dinner. Frances put both crutches under her right armpit and held her drink with the other hand. She struggled toward a seat at the walnut dining table, the scotch sloshing up onto her fingers as she hopped and twisted into position above the chair. She let herself down less gently than she hoped, and the scotch rose up and fell back down into the glass with a moist "plop!"

Frances sat, her bad leg propped up on a second dining chair, and drank her scotch, counting the dark slats in the row of chairs opposite her. She was a finger or two in when the phone in the kitchen rang again. Although she knew that she wouldn't be able to get to it in time to answer, she was glad for the sound. It had derailed a train of thought she didn't want to be on, trying to imagine how to start talking again with her friend Margie. Things hadn't been the same between them since the neighbor boy had his accident in Margie's house. Now Margie spent a lot of time with the boy's little sisters, like she could make up the loss of their brother to them somehow with the company of an old woman. And with Frances not being able to drive for who knows how long, maybe not even leave the house for a while, Margie was going to have to find someone else to take her to bingo, to church. They might not have a reason to see each other for weeks.

As Frances listened to the sound of the answering machine, her eyes shut and she jerked herself up suddenly. Just like that, she had fallen asleep. Maybe she would call Margie. It would be good to talk with someone. She took another drink and searched the backs of her closed eyelids for Margie's number. It started with a four-four, she thought. And then a two. She wondered why in her mind the fours had always been green while the two was light blue. She tried to hang onto the fours and the two while she strained to remember the rest of her number, but they floated off before she could get a solid hold of them. Margie would want to hear from her on the phone. Margie would bring those neighbor kids over and they would eat all her cheese. There was probably cheese stuck to her cheek right now. Not the kid's cheek. Hers. Frances. Frances. The shiny yellow kind that comes in square pockets of plastic wrap that makes a crinkly noise when you unwrap it . . .

"Frances!" Theo was there, shaking her shoulder. She could feel his pointy fingers individually, as if they were sharp tacks about to push through her flesh.

"S'op it, Deo," she said, swinging her arm out to push his pokey hand away but hitting only air. She stretched her eyes open, but they felt better closed so she closed them again. Something was pinching her eyebrow, her glasses maybe, and her right cheek felt wet, but she couldn't pick her head up to see what was going on. She could stay here and Theo would take care of everything. That's what he does.

"Frances! What are you doing? Are you drinking scotch while on the Vicodin? Frances!"

"Deo, sokay. I'm asleep."

"Yes, apparently."

Frances felt the cool night air sweep past her as he left her side. "Deo'll take care of it," she said, her face against the wood. Her head felt impossible to lift, like it was clamped to the surface of the table with a vise. As she moved her lips she felt little scotchy tides move along the edges of her mouth with each syllable. "Deo'sokay."

She heard him in the kitchen. He was talking with someone. Who was in her kitchen? She heard water flowing and she realized that she needed to use the bathroom. Before she could move, Theo was back in the room, his cold hand lifting her head and the other one rubbing the side of her face with a rough towel.

"The nurse says I have to stay up to keep an eye on you all night. Fortunately, it looks like you probably spilled more than you drank, but what a stupid thing to do, Frances. You could kill yourself, you know?"

From the kitchen came the smell of coffee brewing and the hiss of the machine. The acid scent made her gag as Theo held her head up to wipe away the last of the scotch from her neck.

"What? Are you going to throw up now, too?" Through the fog, Frances registered the disdainful tone of her brother's voice.

"S'ut up, Deo. You're not my mudther."

"No, but I'm going to have to be your nanny, apparently. Let's get up." Frances's entire body felt puffed up, blown out with sticky air like a toasted marshmallow, all of her cells monstrously large and fragile at the same time. As he pulled her to her good foot and put her right arm around his shoulders, she felt the wooden floor rise up and snap back in place.

"Deo, I . . ." She lurched forward, catching herself on the table in time to spew lunch all over the top and the tatted runner made by their mother.

"Oh, for crying out loud," Theo said, tucking the damp kitchen towel into the neck of her sweatshirt and leading her across the bucking floor to the couch in the living room. "Stay there," he said, as if she had any desire to move. He propped her leg back up on a cushion on the coffee table and left the room.

The sour smell of vomit mixed with the drifting odor of coffee made her eyes water. She pulled the towel over her face to block out the light.

When Frances woke the next morning, she opened her left eye, only long enough to register that Margie was sitting in a chair near the couch, then shut it again.

"How do you feel?" Margie asked Frances.

"Like a million bucks."

"Well, you look more like a buck two eighty."

Frances groaned. "I feel like someone is punching my eyeballs out from the inside."

"Can I get you something? A cold compress? A cup of coffee?"

"Yes, all of it. And shut the drapes, will ya?"

Margie got up to close the green velvet drapes and then went toward the kitchen, laying a cool hand on Frances's forehead for a second as she went by.

Frances's bladder was pressing against her abdomen like an overfull balloon. She sat up slowly, rocking herself from side to side to gain altitude, then struggled to her feet. Margie had returned to her chair by the time Frances made it back to the couch. A cup of coffee for Frances sat on the table.

"Thanks," Frances said, picking up the cup and looking over it at Margie. Margie's hair had been styled and dyed since the last time they saw each other. Frances wondered who had taken her to get that done. "Thanks for being here. I figured you might be angry at me."

Margie said, "Well, we don't need to talk about that right now." She scooted forward in her chair, pulling on the knee of her thick polyester slacks. She gave Frances a look of concern.

"Stop looking at me like I'm dying, will ya?" Frances said. "So Baby Brother gave up and went home?"

Margie nodded. "How do you feel now?" she asked.

"Like an idiot," Frances said with a wave of her hand, like swatting away the memory of the night before.

"And how does that feel?"

"I don't know. Maybe you should tell me?" Frances said, managing to rouse just a smidgen of her normal orneriness into her voice.

"Aha! There's the Frances I know," Margie said, pointing at her. "You were being so sweet there for a minute I thought the drugs had done more to your head than just make you sleepy." She laughed. "Theo picked me up. He left just when rush hour was over, and made sure I knew exactly when he'd arrive so I'd be ready to go. That way you wouldn't be alone for more than thirteen minutes." Margie looked at Frances and smiled.

"I'm telling you, that guy could run the bus system," Frances said.

"Ain't that the truth," Margie said. The moment of laughter at Theo's expense didn't last long, though. Margie leaned forward in her chair and said, "Frances, he's really worried about you."

"Oh, I'm fine," Frances said, taking a messy slurp from her cup. It was amazing how weak she felt. She set the cup back on the coffee table with a rattle. "I just wasn't thinking. It's not like I'm on Vicodin every day. Those pain killers don't make you feel like you're on drugs, you know, if you're in real pain. They just make you feel kind of normal."

"He was worried about you last night, alright, but I don't mean just that." Margie was biting her lip the way she did just before she said something she didn't want to say. "Theo thinks you should move into senior housing."

Frances grimaced. "Oh, brother. Not you, too. Do you really think I'm going to cram my entire life into some studio apartment that has stained walls and smells like pea soup? What would I do with my furniture? My garden? What about Bean? You know those places always have a nursing home attached. 'Assisted living,' they call it. 'Assisted dying' is more like it. They're just waiting for you to get a little pneumonia or something so they can move you down the hall a little farther. Next thing you know, goodbye, apartment, goodbye, independence. Hello, bedpans and a round-the-clock nurse getting paid overtime to wipe your butt for you."

"Frances, really."

"'Frances, really,' what? You know I'm right."

"Could be. But what do you have here, anyway?" Margie gestured to the room and Frances wished now that the drapes were open. The dark wood paneling that seemed so sophisticated when they moved in decades ago felt gloomy in the shadow. Through the crack between the curtains she could see a beam of fall sunlight illuminating the picture window.

"Who are you to talk? Look where you live, still in Sherman Park, surrounded by those people doing God knows what. I . . ."

"Doing God knows what? You mean laundry? Looking after their kids? Watching baseball on TV?" Margie said. She stood and picked up Frances's cup and her own, stacking them on top of each other.

Frances massaged her tired eyes with her hand. "I don't know," she said. "I don't know what those people do in their spare time. I just mean, you've got to be worried over there."

Margie sat back down, both hands steadying the rattling tower of cups as she did so. "I'm worried everywhere, I guess," she said, a little of the anger drained out of her voice. "But that's not the point. You think that just because you're holed up in your big old house on the south side, you're going to be safe from everything? From life?"

Frances sighed and patted the part of her thigh where the brace ended. The whole leg felt like an overstuffed sausage. "Safe from everybody but the damn cat." She let her head fall back onto the top of the sofa. She could feel the coffee she just drank swirling around, making her a little seasick. Her stomach gurgled.

"Are you hungry?" Margie asked.

"I can't tell. Probably. I could maybe do with some toast." As Margie stood to go into the kitchen, Frances said, "Open the drapes, will ya?"

❉

Sitting on the couch for three weeks was making Frances fat. She couldn't believe it, but it was true. Theo had decided after that first night, when Frances didn't answer the phone and had knocked herself out, that he would move into her house until she could get back on her feet. Theo was a pretty good cook, although he preferred dessert to dinner, and Frances wasn't moving around enough. She sat there, reading, doing needlework, or watching movies. Her big exercise was walking to the bathroom, maybe taking a shower every other day or so. She was filling out; she could feel it in her face and in her waistband.

Frances only went out of the house twice in those three weeks, both times for a visit to her doctor. The church had found substitutes to take care of all of her volunteer duties. Pamela Balistreri told her not to worry, they'd find someone to take over. "Just focus on getting better," Pamela had said, but that just made Frances feel worse, knowing they could do without her. Even Margie was finagling rides from Theo and from Gloria, Margie's black next-door neighbor.

Theo came and went, to his mall walking group and his book club, to the grocery store and the hardware store. Every few days he went around the house with a clipboard, making notes of things that needed fixing, calling repairmen to compare prices. He cleaned out all of the junk drawers and dug into the recesses of Frances's spice cabinet. Frances pretended she didn't hear him when he started shouting about the tin of dehydrated parsley he found that was dated 1983. He even got one of those long-handled dusters that can get the cobwebs out of the corners of high ceilings. He was so annoying, shaking the duster at her every time he went by, showing her the results of his latest conquest.

"You should've gotten married, Theo. You would have made some woman very happy."

Theo stood there in his "grubbies," as he called them—a pair of paint-splattered jeans and a faded brown V-neck sweater—and waved the rag he was holding like someone setting off on a cruise ship. "Oh, yes. Very happy. She'd get clean cabinets and I'd get a closet." He growled this last word.

"Oh, never mind. I was trying to say something nice," Frances said. She could hear the garbage truck banging the carts around in the alley.

Other people were going about their lives, making garbage, picking up garbage. "I think I'm getting stir-crazy here. I need to get out of the house."

"Right now?"

"Yes, now. Let's go somewhere."

"Where?"

"I don't know. I don't even remember what's out there. I don't care. You decide."

"OK, give me just a second."

He went upstairs to change. Frances could hear him talking on his cell phone up there. A stranger, from the sounds of it, because he was using his most formal voice. "Yes, that's fine. One thirty. Thank you. You're very kind," he said as he came down the stairs, Frances's heavy corduroy coat over his arm.

"Do I need that?" she asked, pointing at the coat.

"I think so. We had our first frost a couple of days ago."

Frances hadn't noticed. The roses in the backyard weren't covered yet. She'd have to get Theo to get the Styrofoam cones out of the garage when they came back.

Theo helped her on with her coat, which smelled of cedar from the storage closet. Winter would be right around the corner and she had spent most of the fall watching bad TV and doing cross-stitch. She hadn't been to church or bingo in nearly a month. She missed the annual chili dinner fundraiser at the fire station, too. People expected her chili every year. And why didn't she get the holiday craft fair announcement yet? Maybe Theo threw it out when he got the mail. Or maybe they forgot to put her on the vendor list this year. Out of sight, out of mind, she thought.

Frances shivered and buttoned her coat. She asked Theo to get her hat and gloves from the basket in the hall closet and then they were off, slowly, to the car.

A few blocks away, Frances realized something. "Wait, Theo. I forgot my purse."

"Don't worry about it," Theo said. "What do you need it for?"

"No, go back."

"Why? I locked the house. I've got my wallet. We're OK."

Frances sighed and settled into her seat, but she couldn't make her leg comfortable. The brace was itchy and hot, even in this cool weather, and Frances spent half her energy just holding back from ripping the thing off.

In another week the doctor would take another look. Last time he had casually mentioned the possibility of surgery but Frances had put it out of her mind. "We'll burn that bridge when we come to it," she'd said to Theo on their way out.

She knew what surgery would mean—more weeks immobilized, more pain. More watching Theo measure and patch and dust. At first she had thought he was just trying to be helpful, trying to do the difficult job of keeping oneself occupied in somebody else's house. But then she decided that he was being too purposeful and too quiet to be up to any good.

"Are you getting my house ready to sell?" she said as they rode north along Lake Michigan. The sunlight was reflected off a thousand small waves jockeying in the stiff autumn wind.

"What? Winter's coming. That's a terrible time to put your house on the market."

"You didn't answer the question," Frances said. She stared at him with a hard gaze but he didn't take his eyes off the road.

"I just think you should keep your options open, Frances," he replied, and this time he did look over at her, just for a second, swerving a little as he did so.

"Watch it," Frances said.

"What are you so worried about, Frances?" he asked as he pulled the car back into line. "What would be so terrible about moving into a smaller place?"

Frances's mouth was set like stone as she sat for a moment trying to imagine how to make Theo understand. Finally she said, "What's so terrible? There's a time—maybe you haven't gotten there yet, but you're going to get there soon enough—where you realize that life only moves in one direction. You don't get to go back."

"Of course," Theo said. "Who doesn't know that? I don't see what that has to do with . . ."

"You don't get it," Frances interrupted. "If you let your world get too small, you get small. At some point, you get so small, you're as good as gone." She looked at Theo but he didn't respond, so she gestured to the neighborhood passing by. They were up by the university now, an area full of brick bungalows housing professors and their clever children. "You, you're still out here. You've got a lot of friends. You think things can just go on the way they have been, like nothing's ever going to change."

"Frances, I'm sixty-five, remember? Believe me, I've seen a few things change. And things can change without always making your world smaller. All I'm saying is, keep an open mind." Theo smacked his lips nervously as he steered the car into a long driveway.

Frances turned to look at Theo in disbelief. "Where are we going?" she asked, even as the carved granite sign announcing the Catholic Home came into view. "I don't believe it. You sneaky bastard. Theo, take me home, you conniving little jerk." Right down to the brief trapped animal growl at the end, she sounded just like she did when they were sixteen and six, back when Theo spent his afternoons following her around, hoping to catch her in some misdeed he could report to their mother.

"It's just a visit, alright? Settle down." He pulled the car into a wide spot designated for visitors and came around to open her door. Frances wouldn't look at him.

"Take me home."

"It's just a visit, Frances. Let's just take a look around. Maybe I want to move in here."

"Fine. I'll take me home," she said, grabbing for the keys in Theo's hand. He easily held them out of reach.

"Mrs. Clark?" a perky voice called out.

Frances turned to see a curvy woman wearing the bold red suit of a midrange real estate agent approaching the car and extending her hand. "Hello, Mrs. Clark. I'm Bella Tiergarten. I'm so glad you could come visit us today. How are you doing?"

"Fine," Frances said. "I'm just dandy." But under her breath she said to Theo, "Called in reinforcements?"

Theo turned his back to Frances to shake Ms. Tiergarten's hand, then asked Frances, "Are you coming?"

"Fine," Frances said.

"Good. I'll get the crutches," Theo said, opening the back door.

But Ms. Tiergarten put a hand on Theo's arm to stop him and asked Frances, "Would you be more comfortable in a wheelchair, Mrs. Clark? The entire facility is completely wheelchair accessible, so you won't miss any of the amenities on our tour." Frances already hated this woman's smile. It reminded her of the hucksters at the Mexican airport the one time Chester convinced her to travel outside the country. This woman might as well be speaking Spanish and selling time shares in Puerto Vallarta. On the other hand, Frances was tired already, just crutching her way from the house to the car. Why not let the perky lady push her around? At least she wouldn't have to look at her.

"OK," she said.

"OK! Roger, can we have a wheelchair for Mrs. Clark, please?" Ms. Tiergarten said, seemingly to the air. As she turned her head toward the building, Frances caught sight of a headset on Ms. Tiergarten's ear. The automatic doors parted with a shushing sound to permit a burly guy in a blue security uniform to pass through, pushing an empty wheelchair. Roger helped Frances get settled in and Ms. Tiergarten began the tour.

The place didn't seem too bad. No stained carpets. No lingering scent of Cream of Institutional Food Service chowder. No elderly castaways tied into wheelchairs lining the wall. Or at least, not in the hallways that the tour guide showed her.

"Where do you hide the sick ones?" Frances asked as Ms. Tiergarten wheeled her out of yet another buzzing activity room full of busy seniors.

"I'm sorry?" the tour guide said, as if she didn't understand what Frances meant.

"The sick ones? Where do you put the ones who are too decrepit to take the complimentary shuttle down for Senior Appreciation Day at the public museum? Or read in the up-to-the-minute, fully stocked library with over three thousand volumes?" Frances said, mimicking Ms. Tiergarten's chipper saleswoman schtick.

Ms. Tiergarten stopped rolling the chair and bent down to meet Frances at eye level. "Mrs. Clark, we don't 'put' anyone anywhere. Our residents choose to be here." Something about the tour guide's business-like earnestness reminded Frances of her third-grade teacher.

"Hmph," said Frances as they began moving down the hall again, this time to the heated indoor swimming pool.

Ms. Tiergarten hit the button to open the automatic doors. A warm, moist breeze wafted over Frances. About a dozen women were bobbing in the pool, taking some kind of exercise class. They were all shapes and sizes, some with bathing caps over their hair. The instructor said something that made several of the women laugh, and one of them—a portly woman in a fuchsia suit with a skirt ballooning around her waist—lost her balance and went under. When she came back up a second later she laughed again and gave a goofy, exaggerated wave to the visitors and pushed her white hair out of her eyes.

"Welcome to Water Ballet for Dummies," she called out to Frances, before squeezing the water out of her nose and turning back to face the instructor.

Frances watched the women for another minute while the instructor led them through a partner exercise in which the pairs held hands and took turns extending their legs. They looked like they were having fun. She tried to remember the last time she had been in a pool. In 1984, maybe, when Margie's daughter Nancy got married up in Minneapolis?

The Holiday Inn they stayed at had a pool, so that might have been it. Thirty years was a long time to be out of the water.

As Ms. Tiergarten started rolling Frances back out into the hall, Frances asked, "Do you take pets?"

"I'm sorry, but no," she said.

※

It was a buyer's market, but Frances's Arts and Crafts foursquare with all its original woodwork and glass intact, in cozy Jackson Park, proved irresistible to a nice, professional, thirtysomething man and his "roommate." They threw in something extra to get the Stickley dining room set, too. With a pending offer on the house and a lease at the Catholic Home in hand, the only thing left to figure out was what to do with Bean. Frances put off making a decision until the last possible moment. She had a notice put into the church bulletin: "Free: Six-year-old cat. Gray with black stripes and white boots. Has all her shots. Contact Frances Clark if interested." The Monday after it ran, Peggy Pohl called her. Frances was getting around pretty well, postsurgery. She got to the phone on the fourth ring.

"How are you doing, Frances?" Peggy asked.

"I'm doing OK. I'll get my knee looked at on Wednesday. What can I do for you?"

"I was calling about the cat?" Peggy always had this pleading note to her voice, even when she was offering to do you a favor. Peggy's house would be a good place for Bean, with just a couple of teenaged girls who would be heading off to their own lives soon and a husband who traveled a lot. Maybe Bean and Peggy could keep each other company.

"Oh, that's great," Frances said, already looking at the calendar on the wall next to the broom closet for a good time for Peggy to come by.

"It's not for me. It's for the little girl next door. Her dad is stationed in Afghanistan and won't be home for Christmas. Evie's obsessed with cats and so I asked her mother, Susan, and she said that if Bean was still available, they'd like to talk to you. It would be a sort of a long-distance Christmas present from her dad. Can I give them your number?"

Frances was tempted to say no. She didn't know how well Bean would adapt to a house with young kids. "Are you sure you don't want her?"

"Me? No. I'm allergic. So, can I give them your number?"

"I guess. Sure. Of course."

The phone rang again not forty-five minutes later. It was Evie's mom, Susan. Her voice was breathless as she said, "I hope we're not too late. Am I calling too late?"

So much enthusiasm for a stupid cat, Frances thought. "No, you're not too late. Are you sure you want this cat? She eats a lot. She sleeps where she likes. She doesn't pay attention to you if she doesn't feel like it. She can be a lot of trouble, actually," Frances said, feeling around the edges of her patched-up knee.

"Not to worry. We love cats. Evie's so excited. Can we get her today?"

"Today? I, well . . ."

"Or tomorrow? We could come get her tomorrow night, after I get home from work."

"Tomorrow would be better. I should bring her over to your house. Tell me your address and I'll be there at, let's say, six o'clock." She would have to get Theo to get the cat carrier out and drive them over to Susan's house.

That night it seemed like Bean wouldn't let Frances out of her sight. "Something's up, ain'a?" Frances scratched the cat behind the ears. "You're going to be fine. You'll see."

On Tuesday morning, Frances gave Bean some tuna fish as a sort of going-away treat. "'The Last Supper,' huh? Or 'Breakfast,' I guess." Frances stood watching her eat. When the cat was finished she rubbed her oily little mouth on Frances's shins. "What kind of 'thank you' is that?" she said. "Stupid cat."

In the late afternoon, she packed up Bean's things: her food and water dishes, her felt mouse, a half-empty jug of litter, her brush, the tub of dry food from the counter. Bean examined each one as Frances put it in a cardboard box, touching it with her nose. Theo came over at five thirty and he got the litter box and the scratching post and put them and the box in the trunk of his car. Bean took some coaxing to get into the carrier. She got in when Theo thought to open another can of tuna and put a pinch of it in the back of the carrier on a paper napkin. Frances shut the wire door as soon as Bean's tail cleared the opening.

"Gotcha," Frances said.

Susan's house was close to the expressway, in a little cul-de-sac in one of those West Allis neighborhoods where everyone tries to outdo each other with the Christmas lights. A motorized Santa and three little elves waved their arms slowly up and down in unison as Theo pulled the car up the short driveway in front of Susan's house.

"I guess this must be the place," said Frances. "The welcoming committee's out on the lawn."

Theo carried Bean's cage to the door and went back for the other things. Before Frances could push the glowing white dome of the door-bell, the door opened, flooding the porch with light. Just inside the glass storm door stood a curly-haired little girl, paralyzed with excitement, a smile frozen on her face.

A tall woman in a tunic sweater came up behind the girl and said something Frances couldn't hear. Evie opened the storm door and stood aside to let Frances in, her eyes never leaving the carrier.

Susan stepped onto the porch to bring Bean inside. Theo came in a second later, carrying the scratching post.

"Can I take her out?" Evie asked Frances, her hand already on the latch.

Frances said, "Well, hold on, now. Why don't we try just opening the door and let her come out on her own. She's got to do this on her own time. That's the way cats are."

Evie knelt down on the shag carpet and opened the cage.

"Give her some room," Frances told Evie, tapping her on the shoulder. Evie moved back about half an inch. Frances sighed. "She's not going to come out if you crowd her like that."

"Yes, Evie," Susan said. "Why don't we see what else Mrs. Clark brought for Bean." She led the reluctant Evie over to the cardboard box full of Bean's stuff.

Frances showed them what was inside and then Theo and Evie set up the litter box in a corner of the downstairs bathroom. Theo helped Evie pour the last of the litter in and Evie placed the scoop on the floor, adjusting it several times until it was perfectly parallel to the box. Theo gave her an appreciative glance. "Pretty good, kid," he said.

When they got back to the cage, Bean was gone. "She'll be somewhere dark and warm," Frances told them. Susan and Evie looked under all the furniture on both floors while Frances sat on the couch to rest her leg. Finally, Susan called out, "Here she is. Oh! And there she goes."

Bean came tearing into the living room, whizzing past Frances and then quickly reversing direction. With a smooth leap she was in Frances's lap. She eyed Evie and Susan as they reentered the room and flicked her tail in an agitated rhythm.

"What are we going to do with you, cat?" Frances said to Bean, scratching her under her collar. "This is a nice place, nice people. You're going to like it here." To Susan she said, "Do you have any tuna?"

"Yes, I think so," said Susan.

"Well, go set up her food dish in the kitchen and put some of that in there. Once she's eating, Theo and I will slip out. How's that?"

Susan got the dish set up and then ushered Evie out of the room. After they left, Bean jumped from Theo's hold and sat by the bowl to eat. She looked up warily after each bite.

"Are you ready?" Theo asked.

"I guess," Frances said with a sigh. She watched the cat for a moment more and then called out, "Bean, don't be such a pain in the butt, OK?"

Bean looked up at her and licked a fleck of tuna out of her whiskers, then turned back to the dish. "You know," Frances said to Theo, "I'll probably call later, just to see how they're doing. They might need some advice."

As they made their way to the foyer, they heard the food dish clatter and the noise of Bean's frantic dash up to the second floor.

Theo asked Frances, "Do you want me to go after her?"

Frances shook her head. "No."

"No?" Theo asked. "You sure?"

"She's fine," Frances said, buttoning her coat to go. "She'll be fine."

Menudo

Shit," Bee-Bee said, pulling an envelope out of the dented mailbox on the front porch. The envelope was from her bank and it was ominously thin. Not a credit card come-on or a statement. Just a featherlight slip of paper with the power to knock over the best-laid plans. "What's this 'nonsufficient funds' bullshit?"

She slammed the lid of the mailbox and went to the kitchen, where she dug through the junk drawer, pushing twist ties and old pens aside, until she found her check register. It was true. She had forgotten to put the $200 check she wrote to Julisa's brother in the debit column and her rent check had bounced. Add in the $39 fee for overdrawing her account and who knows what might bounce next. Just when she was getting everything straight.

Bee-Bee threw the notice in the garbage, on top of the remains of yesterday's can of ready-made chop suey. She held the plastic lid open a minute to watch the slippery cubes of chicken turn spots of the page translucent. She thought about calling Netania, her landlord, to see if they could work something out, but decided against it, for now at least. It would be another week before her next paycheck, so what difference did it make whether she called her now or next Friday?

Netania had it made, it seemed like to Bee-Bee, inheriting a bunch of houses from her dad when he died. Bee-Bee dreamed of owning her own house, maybe eventually having a couple rental properties of her own. That would take a while, especially since she needed to make up for what she lost from her time with Jarrett.

She was with Jarrett for more than two years, long enough for him to weasel his way into her heart and then into her credit card accounts. He was charming and a nice dresser, and unlike her previous boyfriend, who was content if they exchanged twenty words in a day, Jarrett seemed to actually like talking with her. He helped keep the house in order and it was nice to have someone to come home to, someone who took care of things so she could focus on her new job as a court bailiff. There was a lot to learn and she tried to keep up with the latest knowledge in her field, studying law enforcement magazines, reading between the lines of the evening news. Soon enough she was trusting Jarrett with more than just a mop and her frequent shopper card. She let him take over the checkbook, pay her bills—their bills, though everything was in her name.

Jarrett had drifted in and out of jobs while they were together, at an office supply store, a diner, the animal shelter. Getting a job was never a problem for him, but keeping one was, so she was glad when he announced he was going to go back to school.

"I'm thinking about going to night school, get a degree in business marketing," Jarrett announced one day soon after walking away from the animal shelter job. "They got a program at Business, Tech, and Trade. I saw it on TV this morning."

"That sounds like a good idea, baby," Bee-Bee had said. "You're a natural. You could sell your grandmother her own false teeth."

She should have known that natural-born salesman was selling her something, too. One day her neighbor, Gina, saw her on her break in the courthouse cafeteria and told her she had seen Jarrett at the casino in the valley the night before, whooping it up with some woman in a sequined dress.

"You must be mistaken," Bee-Bee told Gina. "Jarrett's got class on Tuesday nights." But after work she went home and dug his shirt out from the laundry basket in the closet. It smelled of smoke, and sweat, and somebody else's perfume.

A few days later, her nephew Johnquell had his accident and something broke in her. The afternoon of the funeral, she showed Jarrett the door. Well, she showed his clothes and his stereo the door. He was God knows where, having cut out some time early in the funeral luncheon, without explanation, and just a quick peck on Bee-Bee's cheek. She went directly from the repast to the hardware store to buy new locks.

By the time she wised up, there were bounced checks and over $7,000 worth of credit card charges rung up from all sorts of places, including some recent ones from a west side florist. It wasn't Bee-Bee who got the flowers.

Catching up with the bills kept her busy all fall and winter. Bee-Bee couldn't afford any bad marks on her credit. Her three-year probationary review was coming up and the human resources department was going to look at everything—her performance evaluations from the judges and her supervisor, continuing education records, even her credit report—before giving her tenure. She couldn't let Jarrett, or anybody, mess this up for her.

Bee-Bee had gone to see the credit counselor Judge Mobely was always referring people to. The counselor had negotiated a lower rate with the credit card company and had given her a plan to pay off the $7,000 over time, while still making the rest of her bills. The problem was, there wasn't much room for unexpected expenses, like her niece's birthday or a night out with the girls. Or the washing machine.

Bee-Bee had her own laundry machines in the basement of her rented house, so when the washer conked out in mid-December it was up to her to pay to get it fixed. The repair guy came over and told her labor and materials were going to cost $550. It was an old machine and he'd have to send out special for the parts. It would take some time.

"So, what you want to do?" the repairman asked.

"If the choices are $550 or nothing, I guess it's nothing," Bee-Bee said.

So she started going to the Laundromat once a week, washing her clothes and then bringing them back, wet and heavy, to be dried in her own dryer. She didn't like spending a minute or a dime more than she had to at the Laundromat. The haze of lint in the air and the whiney hum of the machines reminded her too much of being a child, stuck on hot Saturday afternoons with her mama doing four kids' worth of laundry. She used to hang out on the sidewalk out front to pass the time, stepping on ants and trying act like she didn't care that the kids from other families were drinking cold sodas from the vending machine inside. Laundromats were part of her old life, not this one.

Midweek she sometimes resorted to washing a few small items in the bathroom sink and hanging them up to dry on the towel rod. One evening, when her friend Julisa came over for an after-work drink, Julisa went to use the bathroom and came out a minute later with water dripping from her lime-colored nails.

"Girl, you want me to wipe my hands on your drawers or do you want to get me a towel?" Julisa was laughing.

Bee-Bee jumped up and got her a hand towel from the hall closet, then yanked the two pairs of underwear off the towel bar and threw them into her bedroom and shut the door. "Sorry about that. The washer's broke. After washing them in the sink it seems like too much trouble to go all the way downstairs just to hang them up."

"Why didn't you say something? I can set you up," Julisa said, coming out of the bathroom and pulling her phone from her back pocket. "My brother owns Mac's on Center Street. You ever been there? He can get you a used washer for a couple hundred. It won't be new, but it won't be funky. He cleans them up real nice. I'm going to text him right now."

By that weekend, Julisa's brother had brought over the new washer and hauled away the old one—"No extra charge," he said. "You getting the Julisa discount."—and Bee-Bee was back to washing her unmentionables in the privacy of her own basement. Still, she was out that $200.

Bee-Bee knew she needed to make just a little more money, something to give her a cushion to fall back on when these kinds of things happened. So it seemed like a miracle when, the next week, Bee-Bee opened her paycheck envelope to find a notice from the county HR department. It was addressed to the attention of all county court employees and said that if they acquired a working knowledge of Spanish and could pass a writing and conversation test, they could qualify for a pay raise. The judges were desperate for any help they could get dealing with the influx of immigrants to the courts.

"He is an on-time God!" Bee-Bee cried out in the employee lounge when she read the notice.

"Yes, he is," called back one of the building janitors, raising up her arm from the plastic chair where she sat drinking a soda.

"Pray for me, Miss Renee," Bee-Bee said as she got her heavy coat on. "I'm going to need it."

Bee-Bee had taken three years of Spanish in high school, but that was a long time ago. She would need to study a lot to pass the test. She bought a computer course in Spanish and tried to teach herself, but she quickly got all tangled up in tenses and gendered nouns and threw the CDs and their box onto the floor in frustration. What she needed was a tutor, someone who wouldn't laugh at her, just show her where she needed to study and explain the confusing parts, all the *pors* and *paras*.

So when her new landlord stopped by about the bounced rent check, it turned out to be not all a bad thing.

"Hey, I'm Netania," she said, introducing herself under the yellow glare of the porch light one night in early January. The wind blew some snow out of the gutter into her dark hair and she reached up to brush it off with her bare fingers. "I'm Rogelio's daughter and I, uh, own the house now."

"I know. We met before, at his funeral."

"Yeah?" Netania said, cocking her head sideways. "Oh, that's right. I remember seeing you there. Thanks for coming."

"I really liked your dad."

"Yeah, thanks. He was a good guy." Netania fiddled with the leather bracelet on her wrist and said, "So, I, uh, came to find out about the rent. There was kind of an issue. You know?"

"Yeah, I'm sorry about that. You want to come in? It's cold out there." Bee-Bee opened the door so Netania could step inside and gestured toward the couch. Netania was shorter than Bee-Bee, and her sharp eyes and tapered chin combined to give her an impish look.

"You're studying Spanish?" Netania asked. She bent down to pick up the CD cases and book still lying on the living room floor.

"Yeah," Bee-Bee said as she sat on the edge of one of the armchairs. "Trying to, anyways, but I can't seem to follow Señor Montes and Señorita Castillo's directions to the *farmacia*, so I'm just letting them talk among themselves."

They both stared at the place on the coffee table where Netania had neatly stacked the discs on top of the book, as if maybe Señor Montes might have something to add. Then Netania said, "I got a notice from the bank . . ."

"Yeah, I'm sorry. I forgot I had written a check for a new washer and then the rent check bounced and, thing is, I won't have any money for you until next Friday."

Netania pursed her lips and said, "That's the fifteenth. It should be OK. I can make that work. I'll just have to move some things around. It's just, this can't be an ongoing problem, right?"

"Oh, no," Bee-Bee said, waving both her hands at the thought. "I promise it won't be. I'm not like that. I'm just getting back on my feet after a bad breakup. I let this brother pull the wool over my eyes and, well, you probably don't need the whole story."

"No, tell me. I'm interested." Netania leaned over, her elbows on her knees, her open face to Bee-Bee, ready to listen.

"Really?" Bee-Bee said, and when Netania nodded, she asked, "Can I get you something to drink then? A beer?"

"A beer would be great, thanks."

Netania started to get up to follow Bee-Bee into the kitchen, but Bee-Bee said, "It'll just be a second. You can stay there."

Bee-Bee returned with two beers, poured into glasses. "I like your sweater," she said as she set Netania's glass in front of her on a coaster.

Netania looked down and ran her hand down it, a trim sweater with gray and white vertical stripes. "Thanks. It's really old. It was my dad's. He used to be a sharp dresser. He thought he was a real ladies' man, you know? Until Mama got a hold of him, anyway."

"I know all about the ladies' men, believe me," Bee-Bee said. "I don't know how I end up with these guys who still got something to prove."

Netania shook her head sympathetically but didn't comment, so Bee-Bee went on, "Like Jarrett—the breakup I mentioned—he was seeing someone on the side. And from the looks of what he did to my bank account, he loved the slots more than he loved the both of us. I'm working with the credit counselor, trying to fix the mess he made." Bee-Bee looked down at her hands and picked a spot of dirt out from under her thumbnail. "I'm not making excuses, but I feel like I have to level with you. I totally misjudged Jarrett and I'm paying the price and I'm trying to make sure no one else has to."

Bee-Bee held her breath. Netania seemed nice enough. She wanted her to trust her.

"It's going to be OK," Netania said. She raised her glass and motioned to Bee-Bee to do the same. "Here's to ex-boyfriends. And to better luck next time."

They took a drink and Bee-Bee asked, "So we're straight?"

"Straight?" Netania asked. She smiled and raised her eyebrows, like Bee-Bee said something funny.

"Straight. We're good? Next Friday's good?"

"Yeah, we're straight," Netania said, with that bemused look again. "Hey, you know, I used to tutor kids in Spanish at the high school. I can help you if you want." She was turning her glass in her hands as she spoke.

"For how much?" Bee-Bee said.

"For nothing. I'm always glad to help someone learn Spanish. It's important. You can say things in Spanish that you can't say in English, did you know that?"

"Like what?" It had never occurred to her that English might not be enough.

"Well, like, let's say you're on a date, a first date, and you went to the movie and dinner and you talked in the car and now you're taking her back to her house . . ."

"Her?"

Netania opened her hands. It looked like a gesture of surrender, ending with a shrug and a nod.

"Hey, it's OK. I'm not judging, but if you're talking about me, you mean 'him,' and he better be dropping me on my doorstep and not the other way around, 'cause he got the keys to a car that ain't his mama's. I've done that driving-the-man-home thing before and I am through."

"Well, OK. Then I'm on this date. With a woman, OK?" Netania paused, as if giving Bee-Bee time to protest.

"Go on," Bee-Bee said. "You're on her doorstep. What can't you say in English?"

"In Spanish, we have the *subjuntivo*, the subjunctive mood. It means, we accept that we're not in control of every situation, that a lot of what happens is in God's hands. We use it when we don't know how the other person will react to something we do. Like, say that I tell a stranger to do something, then I say it in the subjunctive mood, because how can I be sure if he'll do it just because I say so? Who am I to him?"

"And what about this hot number you left at the door?"

"Well, to her I would say in Spanish, '*¿Deba entrar?*' See, '*debo*' means 'I should' or 'should I?' but '*deba*' means 'I'm not sure if you want me to come in. We had a really good time. We laughed at the same parts in the movie. You like salsa dancing and martinis. I think you like me but I don't know if you "like me" like me, so I'm not sure what you want me to do, standing here, tonight, on your doorstep where it's so cold.'"

"And '*entrar*' means 'go in,'" Bee-Bee added.

"Right. 'And it's raining out here. But only on me for some reason,'" Netania continued. She mimed opening up a tiny umbrella over her own head and tapped her foot a little bit, waiting for this imaginary woman to make up her mind. "'So, still, I don't know whether you want me to come into your house. Where it's warm and dry. And where I'm sure I would be much more comfortable.'" Netania ended her appeal with a sheepish, hopeful grin.

She was cute, Bee-Bee thought. She reminded her of that guy from the silent movies, short with that dark hair and a lot going on in the face. Charlie Chaplin.

She shook her head at Netania's clown act and smiled. "I get it. Subjunctive means not having to guess what everybody in the room is going to do all the time. Lord knows that would be a relief. I need me some more subjunctive in my life."

They looked at each other for a moment and then Bee-Bee finally let herself settle back into her chair. She had been sitting on the edge the whole time.

"What are you thinking about?" Netania asked.

Bee-Bee said, "I was thinking about other ways to say that, that we don't know what's going to happen. I was thinking about my grandparents who came up from Mississippi and how they used to say, 'We'll be at your house for dinner on Thursday, good Lord willing and the creeks don't rise.' I never understood that when I was little. I was like, 'What creeks?' and then I got older and I noticed that we're surrounded by them, those creeks."

※

Netania came to Bee-Bee's house every Monday and Wednesday night to work on Spanish. They sat at the round, four-person dining room table. At first Bee-Bee sat with her chair at a right angle to Netania's, but as the weeks went by Bee-Bee's chair moved closer, like the hour hand on a clock making its inconspicuous migration around the dial. Now they sat side by side, their heads hung over the book that came with the CDs. Sometimes their knees touched, or the length of their thighs, and at first Bee-Bee would jump, but over time that reflex wore down too.

"Sitting Mexican distance," Netania had called it. "It's scientifically proven. Latinos need less space than other people do."

"Why?" Bee-Bee laughed. "'Cause you're all so short?" The difference in their heights, a full head, had been a solid source of ribbing material since the first lesson.

"No, because we smell so good," Netania said, taking a playful whiff of the collar of her pressed white oxford.

"Mmm-hmm. That must be it," said Bee-Bee, rolling her eyes. Netania did smell nice, but it wasn't going to be Bee-Bee who told her so. "For a short person, you sure got a big head," she said before turning back to the lesson.

❉

A few weeks into the Spanish lessons, Bee-Bee and Julisa went out for a drink after work at a new bar downtown near the courthouse. The bar had opened just before the holidays but was already rumored to be the place to be if you were in the market for single professional men in suits. Julisa was keeping one eye on the room while Bee-Bee told her a story about something funny Netania said at their last tutoring session.

When Bee-Bee was done, Julisa said, "You talk about her a lot. You ever notice that?"

"Who? Netania? Not any more than I do anybody else," Bee-Bee said.

Julisa leaned back in the dark leather booth and checked her phone. "Right. So we been here for about fifty minutes and the fascinating range of topics of discussion so far have been 'Where you want to sit?' 'What you going to have to drink?' and 'Netania, Netania, Netania, Netania, Netania.'" Julisa counted these last off on the manicured fingers of her left hand. "Girl, you got a problem and you don't even know it yet."

"What you trying to say? What kind of problem?" Bee-Bee asked. She felt her face flush and her breath catch as she waited. "You want another drink?"

Julisa pointed to her nearly full glass. "Relax, alright?" She gave Bee-Bee a long, hard stare, but there was a light in her eyes, like something was funny. "I just been wondering if maybe you like her."

"Course I like her," Bee-Bee said. "I wouldn't be spending so much time on Spanish with her if I couldn't stand her."

"You know that's not the kind of 'like' I'm talking about."

Julisa didn't look right at her, but Bee-Bee could feel her studying sidelong gaze nevertheless. Bee-Bee didn't like to be watched that way. The booth felt really cramped now and too warm, so she took off her sweater, a pink one with rhinestones for buttons that caught what little light shone on them from the small fixture overhead.

Julisa asked, "I ever tell you my cousin Tammy's a stud?" Bee-Bee didn't answer. "Probably not. My granny doesn't like the family to talk about it. She keeps hoping she's going to pray it away." She put her hand on Bee-Bee's shoulder and said, "But anyway, I don't know what's going on with you, but I just want you to know whatever it is, we're good. OK?" Julisa caught Bee-Bee's brown eyes with her own hazel ones. "It's OK."

"Why you got to keep telling me everything's OK?" She brushed Julisa's hand away, a gesture that came off harder than she meant. "Did I ever say things weren't OK?"

They sat, looking out on the happy-hour crowd, while Bee-Bee racked her mind for something else to talk about. "How about that one there?" she finally said. She gestured with her elbow at a man in a gray suit standing at the bar while she lifted her drink to her mouth.

"You mean the Mexican-looking guy?" Julisa turned back to Bee-Bee and shook her head in mock sadness. "Yeah, you got yourself a problem, alright."

❁

One Wednesday night at the dining room table, Netania shifted in her chair to emphasize a point about *ser* and *estar* and caught her foot around Bee-Bee's ankle.

With the exaggerated concern of one of the voice actors on the Spanish lesson CDs, Netania said, "*¡Disculpe, señorita!*" while looking under the table to see where she should put her foot.

"Not a problem," Bee-Bee said, waiting for Netania to sit back up. Her breath caught up in her chest, but she meant it. She had to admit she liked this, being close to Netania. "I don't mind," she said when their eyes met.

Netania's face lit up with a half smile. "Me neither." She examined Bee-Bee's face for a moment and then returned to the lesson. "Tell me that one," Netania said, pointing to a sentence in English in the "Ordering Food" section.

"'Can you recommend a good restaurant nearby?' How about, *¿Puedes recomendar un restaurante bueno aquí?*"

"Yeah, that's pretty good. The only thing is you don't know this person, right?" Netania said, flipping a page back in the book. "Yeah, see, this guy you're asking, you just met him on the street. So, we don't go saying '*puedes*' to someone we just met, right? It's too familiar. What do you say?"

"I don't know. I'm tired. I say, 'Hey, mister, where can a body get some chitlins to go with all this hot sauce you got here in good ol' Guadalajara?'"

"Chitlins, huh?" Netania laughed. "You like tripas? Maybe we should go to Chivas for some menudo this weekend."

"You mean that place on Sixteenth Street? I always wanted to go in there. It always smells good, but, I don't know."

"But you don't know what?"

"It's like, I don't know, I would feel out of place."

"Not when you're with me, *mujer*. These guys are practically my cousins." Netania put her hand up, saying, "Wait," and squinted with mock effort. "Maybe they are my cousins." She stared intently at the ceiling, like she was making her way through the tangled branches of her family tree. She held this pose just a beat too long, until Bee-Bee laughed again.

"I like to make you laugh," Netania said.

Bee-Bee closed the book and looked hard at Netania. "What do you want from me?"

"I want . . ." Netania tapped her fingers on her own mouth in thought, like a genie had just asked her to come up with three wishes. "I want for you to come with me to Chivas on Saturday morning for a bowl of what you might call chitlin soup and . . ."

"And?" Bee-Bee asked.

Under the table, Netania moved her leg until her knee was touching Bee-Bee's thigh.

"Who could want more than menudo?" Netania said with a shrug.

※

Saturday morning, Bee-Bee got up early. She had been fidgeting in bed since 4:00 a.m., her mind alive with a wordless hum, a thousand bees buzzing in place of language. By five, she gave in to her restlessness and got out of bed. She decided to try to soothe herself with a bubble bath and in the scented warmth she did relax, even to the point of falling back to sleep. She startled herself upright, shaking the stinging gardenia foam out of her nose.

When the water got cold, she got out and got dressed, a pair of blue jeans and a T-shirt, then started some coffee. She tried to settle into her Saturday morning routine a few hours early, but everything she did felt a little bit off. She did some laundry and poured bleach in where she should have put detergent. She went to change the sheets on her bed and knocked over her bedside lamp, denting the shade. She sloshed coffee on the living room carpet. It seemed safer to be out of the quiet house, and by 7:55 she was in her car in front of the dry cleaners, ready to pick up last week's uniforms and drop off this week's the minute the freckle-faced goth girl opened the store for business at eight.

"You're early today," the clerk said, turning to pull Bee-Bee's order off the revolving track without even waiting for the ticket.

This girl always brought on a mild feeling of paranoia in Bee-Bee, like she could tell things about the customers, deduce sensitive information from their clothing. The girl was a watcher, but she wasn't a neutral observer. Everything she did just radiated sarcasm.

"Yeah, I know. I got someplace to be right at nine so I thought I'd come in and get this out of the way."

The clerk turned back to Bee-Bee and cocked an eyebrow. This was more words than Bee-Bee had said to her in the last four or five visits combined. She smiled at Bee-Bee's nervousness. "Well, don't get yourself too worked up," the clerk said as she swiped Bee-Bee's debit card. "It's just a date, right?"

Bee-Bee's jaw dropped. "Oh, no, it's not. We're just going out for breakfast. It's, uh, thank you." Bee-Bee grabbed her card and her uniforms and swept out of the store without saying goodbye. There was a tingling in her stomach that she earlier mistook for hunger but now was realizing was fear.

In the parked car, with both hands on the steering wheel, she asked herself out loud, "What do you have to be afraid of, Beatrice Tibbetts?"

At work she wore a gun and faced down defendants who weighed twice as much as she did. She carried out the orders of judges and protected the jury members. She was tough, but at the moment she felt weak in the knees and sweaty. When her cell phone buzzed in her pocket, she jumped.

"Let me pick you up," Netania said.

"No, I'm not home. I'll meet you, at the place." She turned on the car and looked at the dashboard clock. It was a quarter after eight. She was supposed to meet Netania at the restaurant at nine. "I've got to go change and then I'll meet you there, OK?"

"I thought you liked to be driven around?"

"I was talking about something else."

"What else?"

"A different kind of situation. Listen, I'll meet you there, OK?"

Bee-Bee's hands shook as she dropped the phone on the seat and steered the car away from the curb and toward home. Once there she hung her clean uniforms in the bedroom closet and caught sight of herself in the full-length mirror. She took off her T-shirt and pulled out a blouse she'd been saving for the next time she went dancing with Julisa and put it on instead. The wine-colored material looked too rich against her plain blue jeans so she changed into black ones with silver stitching on the back pockets. She tried on some black pumps and then shook her head. "It's nine o'clock in the morning, girl," she said to herself and chose a pair of low boots instead.

※

Bee-Bee pulled into the tiny parking lot in front of Chivas at nine o'clock on the dot. Netania was already there, leaning up against the side of her SUV. She had on a light blue polo shirt and a tailored leather jacket over it. She was alternating between blowing on her hands and putting them in her pockets, trying to keep them warm.

"Why didn't you wait for me inside? It's chilly out here," Bee-Bee said.

"What, and miss my chance to escort the most beautiful woman south of National Avenue into my favorite restaurant? What would my cousins think?"

Netania opened the restaurant's wooden door and, placing her hand in the curve of Bee-Bee's back, ushered her inside. The touch sent a zap up and down Bee-Bee's spine.

Chivas wasn't much to look at: a long bar with a dim mirror behind it, a set of diner chairs, with vinyl seat cushions in varying shades of greenish-maroon and maroonish-green, arranged around eight or ten gray Formica tables. The walls were done up in wallpaper that probably once was pink, but had yellowed in places where years of shoulders and heads had leaned up against it. In the far right corner there was a TV playing a Mexican music video featuring a band of pot-bellied cowboys with accordions surrounded by cowgirls in fringed bikini tops and sparkly shorts. The cowgirls briefly caught Netania's eye, Bee-Bee noticed, before her gaze shifted dutifully to the Virgin Mary statue wreathed in Christmas lights in the far left corner. Netania gave the statue a nod before turning to the man behind the counter.

"Hey, *compa, ¿qué onda?*" Netania shook the man's hand and gestured to Bee-Bee. "Bee-Bee, this is Martín. Martín, this is Bee-Bee."

Martín looked from Bee-Bee to Netania with amusement in his eye, and let out an appreciative puff of air. Netania gave him a little smile, and then rapped her knuckles on the bar. "The lady's hungry, *compa.* Two bowls of menudo, *por favor.*"

They found chairs at a table for two and before they were even seated Bee-Bee said, "Was he laughing at me?"

"Who? Martín? No, of course not."

"Then why the smile?"

"He's a nice guy. He thinks you're beautiful, I can tell."

"And I'm not the first beautiful woman you've taken here on a Saturday morning," Bee-Bee said and when Netania didn't reply right away, added, "I can tell."

"Hey, are you jealous?"

Bee-Bee felt Netania tap her foot with her own under the table.

"I don't know what I am," Bee-Bee said, pulling a paper napkin out of the tabletop dispenser and using it to dab lipstick out of the corners of her mouth.

"I do."

"Oh, yeah?" Bee-Bee crossed her arms over her chest.

"Yeah. You're a gorgeous, brilliant, strong woman who deserves to be treated with respect, to be spoiled a little bit, to have someone listen to her dreams and help her make them come true, someone who's got her back when she needs it but gives her room to stand on her own feet all the other times."

In spite of herself, Bee-Bee felt tears coming up. That all sounded pretty good right about now.

Netania reached out and put her hand on Bee-Bee's elbow, pulling down the blockade Bee-Bee had created with her arms, and the flood gates opened. Bee-Bee grabbed at the napkin dispenser to try to get the tears before they made a mess of her blouse.

Martín showed up then with a tray with two bowls, a stack of tortillas wrapped in foil, and a long dish with compartments filled with chopped onions and herbs.

He looked at Bee-Bee and said to Netania, "*¿Todo bien?*"

"*Sí, sí,*" Netania said, pointing him back to the bar with her chin. To Bee-Bee she said, "Hey, there, don't cry. What's so terrible?" She stroked Bee-Bee's arm, turning in her chair slightly to keep half an eye on the two muscled guys in denim shirts who had sat down wearily at a table behind her a few minutes before.

"I'm just tired, I guess. I didn't sleep much last night."

"Menudo is just the thing, then, to build up your strength. It's a legendary cure for hangovers, you know? Like these *tipos* behind me. See those red eyes? They're going to leave here ready to move mountains."

"Or at least lawnmowers," Bee-Bee said, laughing a little through the remnants of her tears.

"I'm sorry? What do you mean?"

"It's a joke."

"Maybe it's not funny," Netania said, keeping her focus on opening the steaming foil package holding the tortillas.

"I'm sorry, I just thought, it's a given, you know. You've got a room full of Mexicans, you've got some yard workers, right?" She tried to catch Netania's eye and when she couldn't she threw her hands up in the air.

Netania quit fumbling with the foil and just ripped it open. "You should eat your soup." She wrestled a tortilla out of the mess of foil and waved it at Bee-Bee.

Reaching for the tortilla, Bee-Bee took her first real look at what was in the bowl. "You weren't kidding, chitlin soup," she said, scanning the honeycomb-like parts floating in a deep red broth. She picked up her spoon and held it over the bowl.

"No, wait. Not without a little of this," Netania said, sprinkling in some of the onions, "and a little of this," scattering a couple of pinches of the chopped herbs. "*Buen provecho.*" Netania leaned back in her chair but didn't move to eat anything herself.

Bee-Bee put a spoonful in her mouth, grimacing for a second at the sting of the scalding liquid and then chewing and swallowing a piece of tripe.

"It's good. It's spicier than I thought it would be. It's good." Bee-Bee offered a conciliatory smile to Netania, but it wasn't returned. Some shadow had fallen over Netania's face. "Aren't you going to eat?"

Netania picked up her spoon and began eating.

"*Buen provecho,*" Bee-Bee said.

The rest of the meal passed with hardly a word between them, their silence broken only by various customers' comings and goings. Several times Netania got halfway up from her seat to hug or kiss or shake the hand of someone she knew. When Martín brought the bill, Netania paid right away.

Outside the restaurant, spring was trying to get started, with a blue, late-March sky splattered with clouds. The air was still brisk, in spite of the sun. A harsh burst of wind brought up dust from the parking lot and threw it into their eyes.

Bee-Bee put her hands to her face and blinked until the tears came and washed out the grit. When she could see again, she said, "I'm sorry, Netania."

Netania nodded. "I shouldn't be so sensitive. There are a lot of things we don't know about each other." She took her keys out of her coat pocket and gestured toward her car. "You want to go for a ride?"

Bee-Bee studied Netania's face for a second before saying, "Sure."

Netania walked around to the passenger side of her SUV. "*Señorita,*" she said, holding the door open wide and extending her arm.

When they were both settled in, Bee-Bee asked, "Where are we going?"

Netania thought about it for a moment and then said, "To the lake."

She drove them east and south, not to any of the lakefront parks Bee-Bee knew, but to the port. She pulled up between two warehouses with a large willow growing between them. Netania got out of the car and gestured for Bee-Bee to follow her. The willow looked precarious, its roots gripping the slope of crumbling earth that fell from the asphalt down to the water. Along its yellow-green branches it had only the palest, smallest buds. They stood by the tree and watched the spring wind pick up little pieces of the lake and smack them down again.

"I took my first girlfriend here, in high school."

Bee-Bee nodded. "What happened?"

"Ai," Netania hissed and rolled her eyes. "Did I say 'girlfriend'? I meant 'a friend who was a girl who I was hoping would be my girlfriend.' I took her down here in my dad's car. We were sitting here by this tree, watching the cement tankers go by, and I leaned over and tried to kiss her. Then out of nowhere, she smacks me and goes running. Out there." Netania waved her arm out over the industrial wasteland behind them. "So I had to go after her, of course. I couldn't leave her down here by herself with her book bag and her little school uniform."

"Did you catch her?"

"Not exactly. I caught up with her and rolled down the window and I was like, 'Hey, I'll give you a ride home, OK? I won't try to kiss you again,' but she just kept running. So I drove along behind, like six, seven miles an hour. She was on the track team. Eventually she got to Lincoln Avenue and I figured she knew her way home from there, so I just let it go."

"That's too bad," Bee-Bee said.

"Yeah, I sure learned my lesson."

"What lesson is that?"

"Don't date fast women."

Netania was looking at Bee-Bee out of the corner of her eye. Bee-Bee laughed. Netania laughed.

"So, is this going OK?" Netania asked.

Bee-Bee nodded.

"If I try to kiss you are you going to smack me?"

"I'm not sure."

Netania pulled on Bee-Bee's hand, bending her toward her. "Meet me halfway, will you?"

Pressing On

When they be setting up for Robeson's home-going, Mrs. Charles find me at the back of the church.

"Taquan, how are you doing?" she ask. She got that stiff look she get when she upset. When she angry, sad, or both, her spine lock up like steel.

I don't say nothing, just shake my head. I can't. I got my mouth all twisted up like the cap on a soda bottle. Ain't nothing coming out this mouth.

"It's hard, I know," Mrs. Charles say, patting my arm. "It doesn't make sense. Such a good boy."

I don't got to answer because just then an usher come up to tell us it time to sit down. Both of us about to sit right at the end of the aisle nearby but then Tiana wave us over—a short wave with no real energy to it. Remind me of this pigeon I seen once got hit by a bus, how it flap its one wing 'til it die. So we go up there, to the pew near the front where Tiana sitting. Tiana got those wide, crying eyes, like somebody smack her when she least expect it.

"Hey, Mrs. Charles. Hey, Taquan," Tiana say real quiet when she scoot over to make us room. Normally, she taller than me and Mrs. Charles put together, but today she hunched over with her hands between her knees.

The organist start playing and the room settle down a bit. I look over my shoulder to see who here. The church be packed. Everybody in

here: the football team, all the teachers, most of the senior class, Mrs.
Tibbetts friends, all of Robeson's sisters and cousins. There something
strange about the crowd but I don't get a second to think about it 'cause
the preacher come up before the casket and raise his hands. He old and
his rough, brown fingers remind me of yuca before you peel it.

He say, "My friends, brothers and sisters in Christ, we are here today
for a hard reason. A reason we don't understand. A reason maybe we're
not meant to understand. But still we know, our God is a loving God.
Is that right?"

Some women in the pews call back, "That's right!"

"And still we know, our God is an awesome God."

"That's right!" call the women.

"And still we know, our God is a tender God."

"Yes, he is!"

"A God who lost his own son. A God who knows the heartbreak.
God, our father, who mourns for the way his children suffer. And we
are suffering here today, Lord. We're crying a lot of tears today. Crying
tears for your son, Johnquell."

In the front row, Mrs. Tibbetts got her fist pressed against her
mouth and she make a noise like a grunt, like half a "no." The preacher
look over at her and nod. He say, "Yes, mother, we hear you. We hear
those tears you got locked up in there. We going to try today to give you
a balm for that broken heart." The women on either side of Mrs.
Tibbetts put their arms around her. The choir up on stage stand up and
the organist start up "There Is a Balm in Gilead." The soloist is a woman
in an electric blue suit and shoes to match. She glow as bright as her
suit, like she been asked to sing at a birthday party instead of a funeral.

I don't sing, but the people around me do. In a black church I don't
know the words, but I know most the tunes. Most the time on Sundays
I go with Mami—she Puerto Rican—to the Templo de Dios Pentecostal,
not to a black one like this one here. Pops don't go to church but his
mama, Grammy Fields, drag me to enough weddings, baptisms, and

funerals at Full Faith Baptist that I know the drill. I got my hands on the pew in front of me, keeping my eyes on the stained lace collar of the old woman in front of me. I watch how it scritch back and forth, catching in the ends of her wig hair when she nod to the beat.

I got to keep my mind on this little stuff to keep from walking out while the choir sing, while the preacher raise up his praise hands. Last time I see Robeson he be at the Kmart with Mrs. Tibbetts getting his college stuff. Then a week later, this. Where the balm on that?

I get through it, song after song, prayer after prayer, holding my lips tight, 'til finally the preacher ask does anyone want to say anything and I surprise my own self when I see my feet on the faded orange carpet of the stairs. The preacher hand me the mike.

I see it now, what so strange about this crowd. It about half black, half white, a little of everything else. I ain't never seen that before.

"Hi. I'm Taquan. I went to school with Robeson—Johnquell—I call him Robeson, 'cause, Mrs. Charles she told us about Paul Robeson, that civil rights singer dude—and we ain't never been like best friends or nothing, but we stood by each other, had each other's backs at school. He was real smart, the smartest kid I know, and he funny like, and he be all political and stuff, standing up for what he believe in."

I stop for a second to get my breath and I see Mrs. Tibbetts looking at me then. She smile and nod. It one of those school picture smiles, like she holding it together for the camera, but I see in her eyes she happy to hear anything good about her son. I don't know what all to say but I don't want to disappoint her, so I go on. "I know he was going to do real good at Madison. I ain't half as smart as Robeson but he always telling me I got to go to college too. And Mrs. Charles, our teacher, she been riding both of us about it. And standing here just now I realize I can do that. I can do that for Robeson."

Bunch of people in the pews clap and Mrs. Tibbetts nod hard, with her eyes closed and her handkerchief in her hand. I feel the hand of the preacher on my back as he reach for the mike. My fingers was wrapped so tight around the mike that it stuck to my hand with sweat. I give it back to the preacher and I go down the steps, past a whole line of people—students mostly—who got something to say now too. Mrs. Tibbetts reach out her ringed hand to grab me as I go by.

"Thank you, baby," she say.

I look in Mrs. Tibbetts eyes and that make it realer somehow, that Robeson passed. My arm feel like it turned to stone—my whole body do, all but my face. I can feel my face crumple up and the tears just start shooting out my eyes, like somebody pulled the cork out of the bottle. Mrs. Tibbetts pull me down to the pew and put her arm around my shoulders and I just cry and cry. The girl on stage crying too while she talk and sure enough the whole place just bust out crying.

The rest of the service be kind of hazy. At some point we all go past the casket. Robeson don't look like himself. He all puffed up and they got him in a suit. Inside they put all his school awards, like somebody hoping God got an honor roll. After that we all file out the church, everybody but the close family. When I get to the door I hear Mrs. Tibbetts shout. I turn around and I see her, spread over the casket they just closed, pounding on it, like maybe he going to open up and say, "Just messing with you, Moms," the way he used to.

✴

After the service there a lunch in the church basement. When I get into the dining room it's not too many of those white faces left, but one table got the black kids from Whitefish Bay sitting all together, just like at school. I sit with them—Tiana, Rhonda, Angelique, couple of sophomores and juniors—while we wait for the line to die down. Won't be nothing left worth eating once the old folks get through the line anyhow, so we just sit and talk.

"You really going to college?" Rhonda ask me. Rhonda looking at me with her tiger eyes all crinkled up like she don't believe me.

"Yeah," I say.

"Really?" ask Angelique. Everybody already know that Angelique going to Spelman on a music scholarship. And Angelique know she better than everybody else. "Where are you going to apply?"

I ain't thought that far ahead. I don't even know what I want to study, except I like to run a restaurant some day. Everybody—even Pops—say I'm a real good cook. I do a kind of Puerto Rican/soul food thing, mix it up. But they don't give scholarships to kids want to run restaurants. So I say, "Mrs. Charles she say she going to help me do my applications for next year."

"She still sick. I can tell," Rhonda say, looking over her shoulder to the table across the room where Mrs. Charles sitting with some of the other teachers. We all look then. For real, she been going to treatment for cancer all summer but it just make her look worse.

"She say she would help me anyhow. And you know how she be about keeping your promises," I say.

"'You're only as good as your word,'" Tiana say, stiffening up and tilting her head and pinching up her lips the way Mrs. Charles do when she correcting you. Tiana so good at copying Mrs. Charles, we all laugh. It seem dirty, here at the repast, but we laugh anyway. We can't help ourselves.

🐢

A few days after Robeson's funeral, I go see Mrs. Charles. I ain't got her phone number but I know where she live, up by the high school. I take the 15 up there, watching the houses and yards get bigger and cleaner and prettier the farther the bus get from my neighborhood.

Mrs. Charles house small compared to most of the other houses on the block. It look like the house a little kid always draw if you give him a crayon and say, "Draw a house," with a pointy roof and four windows in the front, two on top, two on bottom. I ring the doorbell and wait a minute, but there no answer, so then I open the screen and knock on the door. Still don't nobody come. I decide to leave her a note. I got a

receipt from the Walgreen's from when I bought Robeson's family a
sympathy card and on the back of it I write:

> Mrs. Charles, I came by to see if you need help with anything. Call me
> please.

I write down my number and stick the receipt between the screen
and the door. I start to walk away and then I get a feeling like maybe I
should take a look around before I go. I go down the little sidewalk that
run along underneath her windows to the backyard. Sure enough, there
Mrs. Charles. She be sitting on the patio in one of those plaid, fold-out
lawn chairs. She kind of slumped over and it make her pink housedress
look like it filled with air. Her straw hat half knocked off onto her face.
My heart stop for a second 'cause she not moving and I think she might
have passed. Then a fly land on her scrawny arm and she brush it off,
still asleep.

There another chair across from her, like she expecting company, so
I sit there. It seem rude to sit down all casual and comfortable when
nobody ask me yet, so I stay on the edge of the seat, with the metal bar
pressing into my legs. I look out on Mrs. Charles yard. She got all kinds
of flowers and little trees up in here. She even got a fountain. It look like
the pictures of the Garden of Eden in the children's Bible my *abuelita*
gave me when I was like four or five. I couldn't read yet—not Spanish
or English—so I just memorized the pictures. In the Garden drawing,
there be flowers all over the place, in colors they don't never come in in
real life, and the trees just be covered with fruit. I wanted that fruit so
bad. It look so good, so red and curvy, like you could just pick it off the
page and eat it. Ain't no surprise to me that Eve couldn't say no.

The closer I look at Mrs. Charles garden, though, I start to see the
weeds popping up. I see a little pile of wilted plants on the grass, weeds
Mrs. Charles must have been pulling up before she fell asleep. It be

getting on noon and the sun be getting hot, but I figure I can pull up
some weeds before I go.

I ain't a hundred percent sure what I should do but then I figure I
can ask myself two questions: One, do the plants look like the ones
Mrs. Charles already got in the pile? And two, do they look like the
plants that grow by my house? My parents don't have time to mess with
a garden. They too busy working. The only thing we do is run the rusty
little push mower over the weeds in the backyard—you can't call it a
lawn—once in a while, especially if we having a barbecue. Once the
food on the folding tables, nobody looking at the ground anyhow. That
be what Pops say and I think he right. He the king of the backyard
barbecue, so he should know.

I remember the first time Pops let me cook—I mean, really cook,
from start to finish. It was my tenth birthday party and Mami wasn't
feeling good and Pops didn't want her breathing all over on the food.

That morning I was laying in my bed, trying to act like I was asleep
but I was too excited to be sleeping for real. I had a real good feeling I
was getting a new bike for my birthday and I was counting the minutes
'til it be OK to get up.

"Taquan," he call me from the hallway outside my bedroom when it
just starting to get light, while he button up his shirt. "You got to get
up. Mami's sick. You going to help me cook or you ain't having no
birthday. Can't let these mountains of people she invited go hungry or I
won't never hear the last of it. You hear me?"

"Yes, sir," I call out but I don't get up 'til he go so he don't notice I
already dressed, right down to my shoes.

That was a great day. I was a smiling fool, cutting up potatoes for
potato salad, running up and down the hall to check with Mami on
how much garlic goes in the mofongo, stirring and stirring Pops's special
barbecue sauce with the whisk he keep just for that. We made food for
thirty people that day. Cleaning up at the end of the party, Pops tell me,

"You done alright. Might just have your mama sit out the next one, too." That much plus the smile he give me and the new bike chained up in the yard felt like I won the lottery.

"Taquan?" Mrs. Charles voice bring me back to the garden, to the here and now, halfway round the yard from where I started.

I stand up and say, "Hey, Mrs. Charles. I came by and saw you was asleep so I started to pulling weeds and I . . ." I stop 'cause she looking at me real confused. "You OK, Mrs. Charles?"

"How long have I been asleep?" she ask, pushing herself up in the chair. The chair start to tip so I run over and catch it. "Oh, thank you, Taquan. You really don't have to . . ." She reach for my hand, but I ain't sure if she mean stop or help her up.

"Can I get you something? Or do you want to go inside?" I ask, keeping one hand on the back of the chair.

"No. But just let me sit here a minute." She tilt her hat so the glare of the sun be out her eyes. Then she take a minute to look around. "You didn't pull any of my flowers out, did you?"

"I don't think so."

"Good. And even if you did, I shouldn't complain, now should I?" she say, smiling at me. "It's not every day you fall asleep and wake up to find your garden all weeded." She get to her feet to have a look. "Nice job. But I'm guessing you didn't come by my house to work in the yard. What can I do for you?"

"I want to go to college," I say.

Mrs. Charles don't waste no time, so she say, "Good for you. Well, alright then. Let's get you started." Mrs. Charles point toward the back door of the house so I follow her inside.

She have me sit down at the kitchen table while she go get something from her office. She come back with her reading glasses and a laptop.

I watch her move around the kitchen, getting us each a soda, and it dawn on me this Mrs. Charles ain't the Mrs. Charles from school. Used to be, when she be doing something, she do it with her whole body, strong, like a tidal wave you can't fight. Now I see she got to focus on every little thing, muster up her energy and put it right on that, like right now on this computer, getting it turned on and online.

Mrs. Charles look at me and say, "What do you want to study?"

"I just want to go to college," I say. I figure once I get there, they going to tell me what to study.

"But why? What are you interested in? What do you want to do for a career?"

Nobody ever ask me that, not in a real way. When you little, people be asking you that all the time—"What you want to be when you grown?"—but most the time it just be something for adults to say to little kids. I guess it ain't all that easy to make conversation with a six-year-old.

"What kinds of things do you like to do?" Mrs. Charles ask.

I try to think of something she going to be happy to hear. It easier when you little. Every shorty know you supposed to say lawyer, or doctor, or fireman, or you want to be the president of the United States. You supposed to be dreaming big, even if there ain't nobody in your neighborhood as big as that.

"I seem to remember you like to cook. Isn't that right?" She scrolling through pages on a website while we talk.

"How you know that?"

"You wrote an essay about it in ninth grade, for Career Day. And I know those Puerto Rican rice and beans you brought last year to the World Food Fest were your own recipe. Rhonda told me they're your specialty."

Mrs. Charles she creep me out a little bit, the way she know stuff about us. But I guess I shouldn't be surprised. She bound and determined to get every one of us integration kids through to graduation and beyond.

"Mrs. Charles, you shouldn't never became a teacher," I say.

"What?" Her eyes go wide behind her glasses. "Taquan Fields, that's rude."

"Naw," I say, covering my mouth with my hand so she don't see me smile. "You shoulda been a spy for the CIA."

She laugh. "Oh, I see. So, does that mean I'm right?"

I nod. "Do they have college for that?"

"Yes, they do. It's called 'culinary arts,' and there's one of the best programs in the country right here at Milwaukee Area Technical College. Do you remember Willa Beekins?" Mrs. Charles squint at me a little bit. I shake my head no and she go on. "Yes, I guess she must have been a senior when you started high school, so maybe you don't remember her much. Her big brother, David, was my student, too, and now he's a guidance counselor at MATC. I think we should give him a call."

Mrs. Charles call Mr. Beekins up right then and, after they chit-chat about how it was back in the day, who married, who got kids, who working for the college, they make me an appointment for Friday.

"You coming with me?" I ask her.

"If you want me to, I will be there." She put her hand on my arm and look me in the eye with her "this is serious" look. "I'll be there, but you need to do this for yourself, Taquan. Not for me, not for Johnquell or his mama, but for you. I can help, but to be successful you're going to have to want it for yourself."

Then she print out a copy of the MATC application and send me home.

I seen Mrs. Charles on Wednesday morning and my appointment was set for Friday afternoon. In between Wednesday and Friday, I got the smackdown from another tidal wave: my Pops. He catch me Wednesday night in my room. He real surprised to see me there, probably 'cause I been out most nights since graduation. Not getting into trouble or nothing, just kicking it with my friends and staying out of Pops way.

"What you doing, Taquan?" Pops ask.

"Working on an application," I say, putting my arm over the paper and turning in my chair toward him. Pops don't like nobody talking to him with their back turned on him.

"A job application? 'Bout time," he say. He look tired, still wearing his greasy shirt from working at the tire shop. "I was beginning to think you was going to be content to eat your mama's food and sleep under my roof and never worry yourself about a dime. You the first person in this family to get your real diploma, but you ain't got much to show for it, do you?"

"It a college application," I say.

Pops come into the room then and pick up my papers and read the first page. "'Culinary Arts'? Cooking? Who need to go to college and pay all that money just to learn to cook?" He look at me. "Boy, you already a good cook, probably a better cook than a real man should ever be. You don't need another paper hanging on the wall just to show off to people. What you need is a job. If you want to cook so bad, why don't you go down the street to Ina's or up to Perkins and get you a job?"

"I can do both," I say. My voice sound small to me, like it squeezing out a bit at a time, like the last drops of toothpaste out the tube.

"Yeah, well, I don't see you working on but one. Tomorrow you need to get out the house when I do and go and look for work."

That be that then. When Pops say "jump," ain't nothing to do but ask how high.

※

Thursday be real hot, one of those end-of-summer days where summer be trying to prove it ain't dead yet. It must have been ninety degrees when Pops drove away from the house with a wave that say, "Get on now," louder than if he yelled it out the window of his Eighty-Eight.

I spend the whole day going from one end of Holton Street to the other, collecting applications and talking to managers who all stink like french fries and sweat. I even go to the big-name chains, even though I know I won't be doing no real cooking at any of those places. One time my boy Hollis, who worked at Taco Bell when we was juniors, show me the color-coded poster they used to teach the new workers how to make all the food. A brown dot mean a spoonful of beans. A green dot mean a handful of lettuce. To make a chalupa you just connect the dots. That ain't cooking. When I walk into Subway and see this girl who live across the street from me—name Adelis, or something—looking like a scrub in her green visor and matching polo shirt, I hang it up. Pops don't know what I be trying to say.

Thursday night I make *arroz con gandules*, Taquan-style—with extra oregano brujo and some smoked ham hock Pops get me special from Big Joe who sells his stuff Saturdays over at the Fondy Market. I pack up a big plastic container for Mrs. Charles so she be surprised when I see her at MATC. Pops be singing Al Green around the house while I cook, 'cause Friday be pay day and also 'cause he like to eat what I make, even if he don't always say so.

The next morning, I get up and get dressed, and leave the house when Pops do. I take the bus downtown and stop in a couple of the diners round there and one of the hotel restaurants, but I ain't feeling it. My mind be on the meeting with Mr. Beekins.

Around twenty minutes to two, I get to MATC and check the map outside the main building. I got my book bag over my shoulder like the students who actually go here, and I try to play out the map in my head so I can walk like I know where I'm at, like I belong.

Mr. Beekins office be off a long hallway with a big sign that say Academic Advising. His secretary say I can sit and wait in a row of plastic chairs across from her desk. I take out the dish of rice and put it on the seat next to me 'cause I don't want to forget about it when Mrs. Charles get here. But the minutes fly by and she don't show. At five minutes to, I start to worry. At two minutes to, I step out into the hall, like I'ma get a drink from the bubbler, and look up and down but she ain't there neither.

When I get back into the office, the secretary say, "You can go in now, Taquan." She got a nice smile. I start to say can she tell Mrs.

Charles where I'm at when she get here, but Mr. Beekins stick his head out the door and say, "Taquan," so I grab my bag and the rice and go over there.

Mr. Beekins a tall, fitted dude, wearing a cream-color button-down with tiny brown stripes and brown pants to match. He shake my hand when I come in and point me to a chair.

"So you know Mrs. Charles, huh?" he say. Behind his head be a bookshelf with a row of trophies on it, look like golf, mostly, but also a couple for basketball, and a plaque from Big Brothers saying he "Big Brother of the Year, 2007."

"Yes, sir. She my teacher at Whitefish Bay. Was anyway. I graduated."

"So we've got the same alma mater. That's great. Mrs. Charles was my favorite teacher, no contest." Mr. Beekins spin around in his chair and get a folder from next to his computer. "Are we waiting on her then?"

I ain't sure what to say. I look at the clock and see it already going on two fifteen. It ain't like Mrs. Charles to let anybody down. You're only as good as your word. "I guess not," I say. I been holding the container of rice on my knees but now I put it back in my book bag.

"That your lunch?" he ask.

"Naw, it just something I brought for . . . it nothing."

"Well, you know, if you're applying to the Culinary Arts program, a little sample of your work might not be a bad idea." He tap his fingers together.

I think, *For real?* so I start to pull the dish back out and he laugh and say, "I'm just playing. Your paper application will be just fine. Do you have it?"

Mr. Beekins and I spend the next hour going through my application and getting all the right papers to the right offices. He take me to Admissions, Financial Aid, the Minority Student Support office, everywhere. He be using words I ain't never heard and I be trying to not let on that most the time I ain't got a clue what he saying. I figure I can ask Mrs. Charles later.

"So, you think you and your parents can fill out the FAFSA this weekend?" he ask when we sitting with one of the financial aid people, a white lady with her hair dyed this crazy yellow.

"What that?"

"This form here," the lady say without looking away from her computer, tapping an orange press-on nail on one of the papers on the desk. "Without that, we don't know how much money your parents can contribute to your education."

"I don't know. I don't know if my dad going to fill that out." Maybe this college thing ain't such a good idea.

"Well, you ask him, and if he's got any questions, he can call me, OK? You give him my card and tell him to call me." She still ain't looking at me.

I leave Mr. Beekins at the door to his office. I got a stack of cards with bunch a people's names on them, more papers to fill out, and a sick feeling in my stomach.

"Taquan," he say when I be walking out. "You and I both know Mrs. Charles is always right about people, right? She believes in you."

I nod. "Yeah," I say.

※

Pops fit to blow when I bring him the FAFSA. "What they need to know all my business for? Just so you can go to school to study something you already know how to do?" He throw the paper back down on the kitchen table. Mami be at the stove, cooking some chicken and acting like she can't see what's going down.

"The college need that so they know how much I need in loans to go to school. The financial aid lady say that most likely it going to show that you ain't got to pay nothing. I'ma get it all in loans. 'Cause we too poor." I know the second that word come out my mouth that my plans is as good as dead.

"Poor? You poor, Taquan?" Pops voice a low rumble, like thunder. He ain't touching me but I can't move, can't look away. His eyes all lit up. "You ever gone a day without a meal? You ever gone to school with no shoes on? Ever been a time when you was sick and there wasn't no money for medicine? You don't know nothing about being poor. Don't you ever try to tell me you think you do." He let go my eyes and turn toward the stove and say, "Mami, I'll be out back."

After he leave the room, Mami come over to the table. She take a quick look at the door to the backyard as she pass it, then sit down.

"Taquan, *mi vida*," she say, touching my face and trying to get me to look at her, but I jerk my head away. "Maybe this idea of college it's not such a good one right now. Maybe you need to wait a little while, work for a while, show your papi that you don't take nothing for granted. He works hard for you, for us. He wants only good things for you. He's so proud of you."

"He proud alright. He be all up in his pride." I ain't looking at Mami but I can see her face in my mind. I can see the little wrinkles in her forehead she get when she worry, see the little drops of sweat on the top of her lip and around the edges of her dark hair from working over the stove in this heat. I know she going to try to get me to do what Pops want and I know if I look at her I'ma do whatever she want.

She put her thick hand over mine. Her gold wedding ring so tight it a wonder her finger ain't blue. "Taquan," she say. In the pause I hear the snap and pop of oil in the chicken pan. A burnt smell be working its way across the room.

"Better watch that chicken," I say. When Mami get up to go look in on it, I get up and go out the front door.

Outside the streetlights is just coming on. I go get the 15 northbound, get off near the high school, and walk over to Mrs. Charles house. Ain't no lights on that I can see, even though it about eight and the sky be turning dark. I ring the doorbell and I knock, too, but nobody come to the door. When I turn away from the house I see some dude standing in his doorway across the street. The light from inside his house be shining all around him so I can't see but his shape behind the screen door. He got his hands in his pockets and he looking at me, watching me go.

The rest of the weekend pass without no word from Pops about the financial aid. On Monday I get a call from the manager at the Hyatt restaurant downtown wanting to know do I want to come in for an interview for a busboy position and of course I tell him yes.

❋

I be sitting on the stoop waiting for Mami to come out for church when I see Rhonda getting off the bus at the corner of Holton and Burleigh. I scoot over there real fast.

"Hey, Rhonda. What you doing over here? I thought you stay on the west side."

"My auntie stays over here now," Rhonda say. "I'm going to her house to help with my baby cousin's baptism party. We got a mess of folks coming over after the church service, so I'm helping get the food and the tables set up."

She point toward Keefe Avenue and we start walking that way. Mami ain't on the porch yet, so I figure I can walk Rhonda a little ways down the street. She be looking fresh in this pink dress that show her shoulders a little bit, even though the weather starting to cool down.

"How's college going?" I ask.

"It's OK." She shrug. "This first semester, it's a lot of review. Next semester I can pick classes I like. How about you? You going to school?"

"I applied to MATC," I say, keeping my eyes on the sidewalk where some kids had drew some hopscotch boards with colored chalk.

"So Mrs. Charles did help you, then. It's too bad, where she's at now."

I quit walking and put my hand on Rhonda's arm to stop her. "What you mean, 'where she at now'?"

Rhonda look at me confused then sad. "She's in the hospital, Columbia St. Mary's. You didn't know?"

I shake my head. Rhonda start walking again and I follow her.

"Miss Snopes said she been in there for over a week and she's pretty much like in a coma or something. She don't even know when someone's in the room with her. This the place," Rhonda say, pointing up to the duplex where her aunt stay. Rhonda put her hand on my shoulder and say, "Taquan? You going to be alright?"

"Yeah, I be alright."

Rhonda reach out to give me a quick hug and I can smell the perfume on her neck. Rhonda's skin the color of honey and she smell sweet too. I take note of the address of her auntie house and say, "I got to get back. We got church. I'll catch you later." I watch her go up the steps and then turn back down the street where I can see Mami waiting on me on the porch.

❁

My schedule at the Hyatt got me working Wednesday, Thursday, Friday, Saturday, lunch to close. It ain't cooking and it ain't the work I plan on doing the rest of my life, but it will do for now. The first few nights I come home so tired I can't hardly get my legs to go up the stairs or my arms to pull open the door. Carrying the dish pans, hauling buckets of ice and water pitchers every which way, moving around the room trying to clear the tables during the lunch rush—I ain't never worked so hard in my life. After the first week, Pops see me reaching into the cupboard for some cereal and he put a hand out and feel my biceps. "You be getting some pipes there, boy. That job gonna do you a world of good," he say and he sound proud, like he the one be doing all the hauling and lifting and running.

I come home near midnight the third week I be working for the restaurant and see a thick envelope on the kitchen table. Look like Mami prop it up special against the napkin holder so I'd be sure to see it. It say "Milwaukee Area Technical College, Office of Admissions" on the outside. I rip it open and pull out the cover letter. "Dear Taquan," it start, "As Dean of the College, I'm pleased to inform you that you have been accepted into the Culinary Arts Associate's Degree Program beginning in the spring semester." I feel my heart jump a little bit, but I push down the feeling. I put the letter in the pocket of my black work pants and go get ready for bed.

✸

At the information desk at St. Mary's I got to tell the lady who I be going to see and I realize I only been calling Mrs. Charles "Mrs. Charles" since the day I met her.

"Vernita Charles?" the lady ask and I remember the one time I heard her first name. It was Mrs. Charles spelling out her name for a cop when Robeson and I skipped out of class and got stopped outside her house. Vernita Charles. The lady give me a clip-on visitor pass to put on my shirt and send me up to the fifth floor.

Mrs. Charles room be in the Intensive Care Unit, so they make me wear a paper gown and booties and stuff, to keep the germs off her, even though it don't seem like I could make her any more sick than she already is. While I be putting on the booties a black man in a sweater vest and tie come by with a paper sack and a soda in a Styrofoam cup. He got Mrs. Charles smile.

"This young man is here to see your mother," the nurse who gave me the booties say. "A former student."

The man look me up and down, set his soda on the nurse desk, and put out his hand to shake. "I'm Henry Charles," he say.

I shake his hand and say, "I'm Taquan."

"You want to see Mama?" he say and I nod. "Come on then."

He walk me to the door to Mrs. Charles room and say, "She hasn't been conscious for almost two weeks. I'm not sure if she knows if we're here, but I think she does. I'm going to sit out here and eat my lunch. You go ahead in."

The blinds be shut and the room be kind of dark, but I can see she on the bed, flat on her back. She so skinny by now that she hardly make a bump in the covers. Her green glasses be on the little table next to the bed, folded shut like she ain't used them for a while. Next to the table be one of those IV stands, with a tube running down into Mrs. Charles right hand. I sit down in the chair on the other side of the bed. I don't know what I'm supposed to do so I just stay like that for a while, just watching her face. Then I remember the letter. I get it from my back pocket and open it up.

"You told me to let you know when I heard something from MATC. I don't know if you can hear, but I'ma read this to you. OK, Mrs. Charles?" I wait a few seconds like she going to answer back and then I start. I done read this letter so many times that even in the shadowy room I can read it clear as day. When I get to the end, where the Dean of the College say "Congratulations once again," I tell her, "I'm going to college, Mrs. Charles, soon as I have the money saved up. I got a job, at the Hyatt restaurant downtown. I been working there for a few weeks now. I'm just the busboy but I think the cook, Marco, going to let me start helping in the kitchen now and then. Just little stuff, like prepping the vegetables. He see I be watching him all the time when the lunch rush be over. I told him I'ma go to culinary arts and he tell me when I start he going to show me some things. He went to MATC, too. I need to get my Pops to fill out the financial aid form though. He don't want to. He say it make us look like we poor. He too proud to take the help. But I think, everybody need a little help sometime."

She don't say nothing to that, of course. I be missing her voice real bad then. It kind of hard to wrap my mind around the idea that this little bump in the covers be Mrs. Charles. For a second, I get this crazy picture in my head that the real Mrs. Charles be out in her garden somewhere, and this one here just a fake.

I been keeping my eyes on her face but I look up when I hear somebody by the door. It Henry, listening to me go on and on. I don't know how long he been there.

Henry say, "I think she hears you."

"Why you think that?" I ask him, looking at her on the bed and then back up at him.

He say, "She's been breathing faster while you've been talking to her, like she's excited about something."

I ain't been paying no attention to her breathing, just watching her face hoping she would open her eyes.

"That be just like Mrs. Charles, I guess. Even when she so sick she still be getting all wired about kids going to college."

Henry laugh. "Yeah, that's Mama."

I give Mrs. Charles hand a squeeze and pat her shoulder as I stand up. "I better get going," I say.

"Wait a second," Henry say. "Why don't you give me your phone number, in case we get some news. We've been keeping Miss Snopes at the school informed, but I can let you know too."

I tell him my number and then I got to ask, "You a teacher too?"

Henry laugh. "Is it the vest?"

"Yeah. And, I don't know, you just feel like a teacher."

He nod and say, "You're right. Apple didn't fall far from the tree. I teach math in Brown Deer."

I look at him. He got those sharp but nice eyes just like Mrs. Charles. "I bet you're a good one," I say.

Henry point at his mom. "There's the really good one, there."

I ain't surprised when I get a call just a few days later saying Mrs. Charles passed. Didn't seem like when I visited there be much more of her left, just enough body to breathe and to wait.

What do surprise me after the home-going—which be just as bad as Robeson's, I mean, I ain't trying to go to no more funerals—is the envelope that come in the mail a couple weeks later. Just like before, Mami prop it up on the kitchen table so I don't miss it when I come in late from the restaurant. The envelope got the name of a law office on Buffalo Street.

At the top of the letter inside it say, "In re: the Estate of Mrs. Vernita Martha Charles née White," and the letter itself start out, "Dear Mr. Fields." It go on to say that Mrs. Charles leave me $3,000 in her will. Inside be a check for the full amount. That enough to pay the first two semesters almost. If I keep working and saving my money, I can pay for the next year myself.

"What does the letter say, Taquan?" Mami's voice make me jump. She standing at the doorway to the kitchen in her nightgown and *chancletas*. It don't look like she been asleep though.

"Mami, why you up? You going to make yourself sick if you don't get your sleep."

"I can't sleep because I am wondering why my son is getting a letter from lawyers. Are you in trouble?" She put her hand up on the wall like she trying to keep from falling over.

I got to laugh. She ought to know after all these years that I ain't the kind of kid gets in the kind of trouble needs lawyers. Worst thing I ever done is skip out of school early a few times with Robeson. "Naw, it a check. Mrs. Charles left me some school money in her will."

Mami come over then to take the envelope out of my hand. She try to read the letter but in the little bit of light from over the sink she can't without her glasses. She can read the numbers on the check, though. "Three thousand dollars, Taquan? We can't accept this. It's too much."

"It a gift, Mami. Mrs. Charles really wanted me to go to college. She believe in me. She think I'ma be a great chef someday."

"But what about her own children? They don't need this money?"

I think about Henry in the ICU. He look like he doing just fine.

"Mami, they all grown. Besides, Mrs. Charles a smart woman. She ain't going to give away money her kids need."

Mami put the check back in the envelope and hand it to me. She pick up a dish rag and start wiping down the faucet and the edges of the sink with it. "Don't tell your father about this check. Tell him you're going to pay your school with money from your job, that you made a special arrangement with the school office, OK?"

In the light from over the sink, Mami hair glow like a halo around her face and she do seem like some kind of angel to me. She and I both know Pops going to make me take that check back—to Henry or to the lawyers or somebody—if he know about it. He just too proud for his own good.

I can't think of no other time in my life when Mami ask me to keep a secret from Pops, not a real secret like this anyway. She always be holding her finger up to her mouth and warning me "*no digas nada*" about silly stuff, like what she be making him for his birthday dinner or something like that, something he going to be happy about. But maybe this going be something like that after all, in the long run.

The check settle another question beyond how I'ma start paying for college if Pops won't fill out the paperwork. When I be planning out my restaurant I can see how it all going to be—what the food like, what color the chairs is, everything—but I couldn't never settle on a name. Now I think "Vernita's" sound about right.